AKILAH TRINAY

# BEYOND THE HURT

EDUCATION·COURSES·RESOURCES

First published by Revision Publishing LLC 2016

Copyright © 2016 by Akilah Trinay

This novel is entirely a work of fiction. The names, characters and incidents portrayed in it are the work of the author's imagination. Any resemblance to actual persons, living or dead, events or localities is entirely coincidental.

Designations used by companies to distinguish their products are often claimed as trademarks. All brand names and product names used in this book and on its cover are trade names, service marks, trademarks and registered trademarks of their respective owners. The publishers and the book are not associated with any product or vendor mentioned in this book. None of the companies referenced within the book have endorsed the book.

Second edition

ISBN: 9780692566558

Editing by Nicole Walker
Cover art by HotBookCovers.com

This book was professionally typeset on Reedsy.
Find out more at reedsy.com

*This book is dedicated to my parents; family, friends, loved ones, and students who dream of making something happen; take the leap of faith and do it!*

# Acknowledgments

All glory belongs to God! Who is truly the head of my life and is the reason why I live and breathe. He has blessed me with a loving family; friends who keep me lifted and encouraged every step of the way, and a praying church family. However, I have to personally thank my mother, Trina Norris, my father, Andrew Spider Norris and my sister, Tabia Norris. They have been the absolute backbone to this project and without them I am not sure if it would have happened; from reading the manuscript, to designing logos, to pitching in funds. I love you beyond...

Taking on this task was not an easy one and I have one person who took me from a place of talking about writing this book, to actually making it happen. Michael McGrew has been my inspiration through this entire process. His writing success was the blueprint for me and he literally provided me with the blueprint that he published himself (wink wink).

To the few who read a chapter or the entire story: Breya Harden, Marilyn Barnes, Dominique White, Delores Fractious, D'Angelo Tate, Cierra Hudson, Dontrail Hunter, Ky'Onna Jacobs and Sonja White; your input and time spent is much appreciated.

My most heartfelt thanks are to my financial backers: Anton McCall, my brother from another mother; Stephanie and Fletcher Brown; Nicolas Keen Swearingen aka Nic-Nic; Sir Jade Pope; Josette Tippens and family; Vanisha and Terrence Boyd Jr.; Felicia Brown, Love Luv; Chante'l Williams and Bhati Gant; Andre Anderson; Kori Boxdell (you are truly amazing!); Alma and Stan McKenzie; Latina and Rick Fortenberry; Etta Brown; Andrea Jones; and Aunt Gloria. These individuals along with countless others helped to fund this project. They believed in me and for that, I am forever grateful. For every prayer, FB share, Like, Repost, and encouraging word: Thank you. Thank you. Thank you!

Dear Readers:

Please sit back and enjoy the ride that you are about to embark on; journeying through the lives of three families that are far from perfect. The families represent our struggle sometimes with trying to take life into our own hands, allowing the enemy to distract with the pride of life, and not allowing God to be in control. You will find that there is some vulgar language throughout the story to maintain the integrity of the characters. Reader discretion is advised.

# Prologue

Debra Tucker
  February 27, 2010
  English 101
  Professor Greene
  First Draft Narrative Assignment

My Life - Evolution of Man

**Evolution** - noun

*1 the process by which different kinds of living organisms are thought to have developed and diversified from earlier forms during the history of life.*

A man has to fight for his freedom. Although, as a woman, I understand this concept. Each and every blow translates strength. He is a warrior. He lives to share the story of his battles, showing the wounds to his companions, earning him stripes, credibility, and respect within the community. He lives. But what happens in war? People die. Innocent people die; families are destroyed for the sake of power and survival. Life, liberty, and the pursuit of happiness is money.

Every human being in America is in search of money by any

means necessary. Some take handouts; others work hard and never play. While others take what they believe belongs to them. Daily, there is a grind, a hustle to be successful, to be loved, and to stay on top. Money. Power. Respect. If this were a fraction, the common denominator would be women. Can't have a life without a woman, right?

My story is simple. Structured in a way to make people listen every day, I didn't realize my story started before I was even a thought. I lived this life before. My brother Samson was born dead in more ways than one. Society says that a Black man doesn't stand a chance in the urban community beyond the age of eighteen. The murder rate amongst young black males agrees. But my brother was literally born dead. He didn't cry, not a peep. My mother was hysterical and in almost a blink of an eye, he took a breath. He opened his eyes. Samson took on that persona for his new life. He makes his own rules; he dances to the beat of his own drum.

It seemed odd to me that we were related and born of the same flesh. I was born alert, aware and curious. Eyes wide open, understanding and questioning at the same time. However, our worlds were different, yet the same. Our experiences were disconnected but connected. Charlene and Edmond were to blame. The two that came together in love multiplying it by two. Charlene Tucker understood her husband. She was aware of the support she needed to provide him with knowing the black man's daily struggle to do right by his family by being financially supportive, staying faithful to his vows and providing a well-balanced, structured environment for a family to thrive. If it was only that easy, but it was something you would definitely have to be built for.

**Survival of the fittest (Biology)** - *The continued existence of organisms that are best adapted to their environment, with the extinction of others, as a concept in the Darwinian theory of evolution. Compare with natural selection.*

**Natural selection** - *The process whereby organisms better adapted to their environment tend to survive and produce more offspring. The theory of its action was first fully expounded by Charles Darwin and is now believed to be the main process that brings about evolution.*

A man teaches his son the best he can to survive in a world that wants to eat him alive. A world where his success is not celebrated by the masses but instead is hindered. If there is no father present, then the son has to make do the best way he can. He finds prominent figures in the community to imitate, but not everyone makes the best role model. The hope is that if one doesn't make it to the destination that they saw fit for their life, their offspring, their legacy will continue and eventually make it to that Promised Land.

Note to self: Make sure I finish this assignment.

# Chapter 1

"I never thought we would see the day," Charlene sighed as she gazed into her husband's dark, tired eyes in between shuffling boxes around. "Edmond, our baby is going to college." Edmond Tucker rested in his smoky-brown, one-man Lazy-Boy recliner, sipping his chilled Miller Genuine Draft, his morning pick-me-up. He was too tired to give his wife a response, taking a break from all the packing. "At least one of our children will go on to be successful and carry out the family legacy." She continued, as if knowing her husband would maintain his silence as he often did when she carried on her rant about the children. "I just get so worried about Samson. Out all hours of the night, no actual job. You know it is not safe in the streets. And not to mention, he just mooches off of us. We are enablers, honey."

Edmond sat anchored, flipping back and forth through the sports and cooking channels. Her endless tirade agitated him to his core, especially in moments of relaxation.

"Stop complaining, woman!" Edmond finally broke his silence, shifted his body upward, disappointed that he had to leave his posture of comfort to address his wife. He slammed his half-finished bottle down hard on the hardwood floor adjacent to his chair, luckily avoiding a shattered mess. "That boy is finding himself, like every other man must do in this life. He ain't no different from me when I was his age. You remember? You had no problem hanging on my coattail then. You liked that part about me." He paused to gaze in her direction for confirmation. "Let's just be proud that he is still alive, and he has the decency to love and respect us and hasn't given us any extra mouths to feed. It could be worse." He rested his case and sat calmly back in the chair, hoping his wife would take that and leave him in solitude. He steadily had to remind her that the son that they gave birth to twenty years ago was still immature, but evolving as a man in his timing.

"I guess you're right, dear. But you were definitely hounding me back then. Get it straight!" Charlene spoke quickly to ensure her husband that she was listening and didn't want him to get all worked up. It was difficult for her to adjust to Samson being so independent, refusing her motherly advice and nurture. He was a licensed mama's boy; but to her dismay, he was drifting away. "But that is my baby and…"

"Charlene Baby…not another word." Edmond didn't budge this time; he just raised his hand to command silence.

"I think I am all set to go," I said, interrupting them from their intense conversation about my no-good brother. He always knew how to be present while being absent. Many of their heated arguments centered on Samson and the hopes and dreams my mother had for him and how he frequently managed to disappoint her. My mama was very naïve when it came to Samson; he constantly played on her emotions and she just let him. She was clueless to the fact that he was no longer the little boy that would run and jump in her lap or ask her to kiss his wounds so they would magically feel better. It was quite sickening if you ask me. She never gave me that much time or energy. I guess you can say I longed for that type of attention. I was a young girl with questions, curiosities, and it was rare that I even found comfort in discussing them with my mother. My father, on the other hand, was the best support system I had. He was genuine, strict, but I knew he had my best interest at heart.

My older brother, Samson Tucker, is a highly intelligent man, strong and athletic, but extremely lazy. From the time he was a little boy, he relied on his witty charm to get by. He frequently skipped class avoiding any homework obligations, but he would magically pass all of his classes with a C average. He would even receive high reviews of his potential and guaranteed success if he only *"put his mind to it,"* as Mr. Garren, his English teacher, would say. I believe he paid all of his teachers off or promised them discounts at NUMMI, since our father worked there and was referred to as the "HNIC," knowing our dad wouldn't even give his own mother a discount if she was stranded on a deserted island with no bus pass. And I am well aware you cannot take a bus off an island.

New United Motor Manufacturing, Inc. (NUMMI) was an automobile manufacturing company jointly owned by GM and Toyota. My father commuted every day to Fremont knowing that he was well valued at the company, being that he was part of the decision-making team to have the plant reopen and focus their production on high-quality, profitable small cars manufactured in the United States. He generated an abundance of revenue for the company. So yea, we were your typical middle-class family, not rich, but definitely comfortable.

Samson has charm. It is undeniable. His ability to control the minds of people is unnerving. He is a certified manipulator, but I don't blame him, he got it from Mr. Tucker. My dad was the gentle gangster type, a smooth Mack-daddy. I know he had all the ladies back in the day. I once stumbled across his high school yearbook; all his special messages were from the ladies: *Hey Big Daddy, Have a nice summer Cat Daddy.* It was actually very disturbing to read, imagining that my father having any type of sexual encounters or women flocking to him in that way.

Yet, I wasn't surprised. Women constantly threw themselves in my father's direction, even in the presence of my mother. She attempted to save face and appear, as though it didn't bother her, but I know deep down it was a struggle for her. They met in community college and spent several years getting it together, understanding one another and how to make a relationship work. He *is* handsome though, my father, that is. Women swooned over his milk-chocolate skin tone and salt and pepper hair with more salt on the sides than pepper. My mama had a good catch, a good-hearted man, and a great father.

Unlike me, Samson had no desire to attend a college of any kind. Be it community college or trade school. He enjoyed his daily hustle. In his mind, he was living the "thug life." This was obviously not the case. He couldn't even withstand his first tattoo session because he claimed the needles weren't clean, the first prick he was claiming that he may be infected. As a result, he lacked the tats, the gun and the baby mama. What type of thug do you know in Oakland like that? He basically lacked the "thug" requirement. Now "Thug Life 101" states that at the very least, you must tote a gun. However, he assured me that after his next deal went through; he was going to buy a .45 from one of his boys who had hookup on artillery.

We lived in a quaint neighborhood on the east side of Oakland. There was not much criminal activity that took place beyond the occasional bike theft or break-ins, so Samson went out looking for commotion and activity. He yearned for street credibility; he wanted to earn his stripes. In my opinion, Samson was far from possessing "swag" or the guts to use a gun, but living in Oakland, I knew why he would need it.

"It is definitely time to go." I announced to my parents to get them moving. I had everything possible from the house I could think of packed, stuffed, tucked away in plastic bins, bags, suitcases, and boxes. My parents and I would be taking the drive down to the University of California, Riverside. They promised to help me get acquainted with the campus and get everything situated in my dorm room. The truth is, my father wanted to make it known to any male specimen on the campus that if they even attempted to look in my direction, they would be subject to deal with him personally and forfeit any opportunity to live to tell another soul about the encounter. My father was one hundred percent serious about me not dating. For most girls my age, their fathers would, at the very least, give them the "wait until you turn 18-and-you are grown speech," but no, not Mr. Tucker. He believed that as long as I was his precious baby girl and as long as blood was pumping through my veins, I was not to even look in the direction of any man, young or old, especially old or older than me. That is, unless he selected him and he measured up to his standards; which was relatively no one.

My father was beyond overprotective. He hardly ever let me date and if I did manage to manipulate him into letting me go out to a movie with a guy and some of my girlfriends, in the afternoon on a Saturday, he had to meet him. He was required to fill out a two-page form including his address, social security number, nicknames (just in case he had to ask around the neighborhood), parents' names and contact numbers (home, cell, pager, AIM, email, etc.) I think my father was a private detective or police officer in a previous life. Nonetheless, I was forced to sneak around if I was to have any chance of a relationship or a life. If he ever found out that I lost my virginity just two weeks before I made the decision to move to Riverside, he would have me slaughtered. He wouldn't be able to live with the fact that his baby girl was not as innocent as he assumed, and his protective measures were not foolproof.

"I am so proud of you, Debra," my mom cried, tears rolling down her face, smearing her well-applied makeup. She stayed in full makeup at all times, not because she was an unattractive woman, but because she knows what my father likes. She is all about keeping her man happy and satisfied. "I remember just the other day, the first time I looked into your almond brown eyes, not knowing a thing about what this world would bring, and look at you now, seventeen, beautiful, intelligent and going to a university. The first in the family all grown up and making us proud." Suddenly, her tears mighty-morphed into anger, transforming her skin from a cinnamon brown into a swampy dark green, as if The Hulk was staring dead in my direction. Out of the corner of her eye, she caught a glimpse of the box I did a poor job of hiding. "I know you are not taking my new cookware out of this house!" *Busted*. Charlene Tucker had a good way of making a special moment sour in an instant. "What else do you have in these boxes of mine?" she demanded. Little did she know; I packed several of her household items in my plastic containers. A girl needs supplies to live. I was going to college, and she clearly didn't need it. I felt that if she hadn't used it up until now, it was just like mine.

"Let the girl alone!" my father interceded. *Saved.* "The more she takes now, the less money she will be begging for later, and as much crap as we have in this house, I am happy for her to take it off our hands." Most of the items my father helped me package; he knew his wife was a hoarder. Every sale she saw as an invitation to add items to her home collection. Charlene could open up an emporium right in the center of Downtown Oakland, if she played her cards right.

I noticed my mother's expression slightly change as her skin transitioned back to its normal coloration. "You are right, Babe. I am overreacting," my mother said, surrendering. She rubbed the top of her husband's head, as she often did, to calm him down, soothing away his frustration.

*Like always*, I thought to myself. *Part of the reason I want to get away.*

It was already noon and time for us to get on the road if we wanted to make good timing. Interstate 5 was not friendly at certain times of the day. We loaded up my father's extra-large navy blue 2009 Toyota Tundra truck with its V8 engine, what he referred to as his mobile man cave. When Mrs. Tucker gave him just too many words or too much attention, he was off and away to clear his mind. NUMMI made sure to keep my daddy laced in the newest trucks. Whenever he wanted to trade his old truck in for a newer one, all he had to do was ask, sign on the dotted line and it was his. After 25 years of service and dedication, he more than earned it. He was the sole reason why NUMMI was able to keep from going under and shutting down. He had special connections with all the big business bosses. He had friends in high places who owed him some favors, and naturally, he called on them. He was literally the

7

man at work and around town. He often tried to get Samson to fill out an application to earn some legitimate income and become a working man, but Samson refused, quoting Trick Daddy *"Baby because I'm a Thug."* As a man, Samson didn't want handouts from his father. He wanted to get it on his own.

As the engine began to rumble, we placed the last of my life in the rear of the truck. The quick packing process turned into a two-hour project, with me running back and forth in and out of the house, ensuring that I had everything.

"Honey, are you OK to drive? I know you had a beer and I don't want to have any accidents on the road." Charlene was concerned that he could potentially put them in harm's way.

"I've been drinking all these years and today you ask if I am OK?" Edmond responded with irritation. "I only had a few sips because I knew I would be driving, but if you want to drive, you can go ahead."

Edmond knew that Charlene would never offer to drive his truck. She didn't trust herself to even drive it sober they would be better off with him chauffeuring in his condition. "No, babe, I trust you to keep us safe," and we set off on our journey down to Southern California, leaving Samson behind to get into nothing but trouble as usual.

I felt the truck coming to a stop. I had barely closed my eyes for what seemed like a minute, but I was certain we had not made it to Riverside. It made no sense to me why we were stopping and we literally just got on the road. My dad mentioned receiving a call from a client who had some sort of accident in one of their vehicles and had to run by the courthouse to pick up some paperwork. How the accident and the courthouse connected was beyond me, but I learned a long time ago not to question his movements. My mother was just as sensible. She rested on every word he said and took it as fact, unless it was about her beloved Samson.

We pulled up to the Alameda County Courthouse and my dad hopped out, actually he more like slowly hobbled out of the car and told us to sit tight while he went in to take care of business.

"Daddy, please don't have us waiting too long," I whined as he motioned to shut the door. "I'm ready to get to Riverside. We don't have time for this."

"Girl, there would be no U.C. Riverside if it wasn't for yo' daddy, so sit back, shut up and let yo' daddy handle his business."

Of course, Charlene had to interject with her, "my man is the almighty *Mandingo* rant!" My mama had her ways and all of them ended on my nerves. I knew we had a six-hour drive ahead of us, so I decided to concede and allow her to win this one. I put my seat back and slapped on my headphones to drown out her nagging voice as I mellowed out to my favorite album, *The Miseducation of Lauryn Hill*.

# Chapter 2

The salon was fairly empty for a Friday afternoon. Although most of the clients were required to schedule an appointment, the weekend initiated an influx of women determined to rectify their hair disasters in time for the weekend sun and activities that they hoped would elevate their social and relationship statuses.

"Tanya, how many more appointments do I have for today?" Raquel moved about the salon, sweeping and wiping down her station. It was still early for her pre-weekend appointments; she had been up working since six in the morning. Friday was the day that most women wanted to get into the shop to be alluring for the weekend festivities or impromptu trips to Las Vegas, Los Angeles, or Lake Tahoe.

"You have Jenise at 2pm coming in for a relaxer and wrap and Miss Juanita at 4pm for her roller set." Tanya replied with conviction, not once taking a glance at the appointment book, while she filed her low-cut almond-shaped nails at the receptionist's desk located at the entrance of the shop. Tanya was in the process of completing her cosmetology hours in hopes of one day becoming the owner of her own salon. She had been apprenticing under Raquel at her salon for the past month. The little diva was on it. Tanya knew that working for Raquel was the best thing she could ever do, an once-in-a-lifetime opportunity. All the little girls in the city who finished beauty school wanted to work under her. She knew she had to bring her A-Game every day. It was mandatory for all of Raquel's girls to go through a rigorous initiation. Teaching them the process of proving themselves through hard work and dedication, she ran all the errands from Sally Beauty Supply and Keisha's Hair Care Warehouse to quick fixes, like CVS. It was essential for her to schedule all appointments, wash and prep clients for the entire stylist team. Raquel and all her stylists never failed to whip all their clients up and send them on their way looking drop dead-gorgeous!

"Good! I can rest my feet for a while until Jenise comes in. My dawgs are barking!" Raquel yanked off her LifeStride Klarissa pump, gently massaging her foot moving between the ball and heel. The high and low lights, accent walls and wall decor gave her salon the much needed calming essence many of her clients appreciated when sharing their innermost secrets and gossip during each hair session. The shop was located in the quiet middle-class neighborhood of Piedmont. Raquel wanted her clients to travel outside of their comfort zones in more ways than one. She selected this particular location because it spoke of affluence and accessibility. It wasn't Oakland, but it lay just adjacent to her home city right on the border; so no one could dare to call her a sellout.

Raquel slumped down in the cozy black salon chair. This was her place of solace. Everybody knew that when she was in her state or relaxation, to leave her alone. They especially knew that when she was in the V.I.P. *"Vixens in Preparation"* chair, it was game over. This particular chair was only for her top-notch clients who didn't mind paying a few hundred dollars

11

extra. As her girls would say, everything she did was high-class-bougie. She offered manicures, pedicures, waxing, and facials. She even had a to-go or dine-in food service with any type of food offering desired. Her goal was to have all clients to feel pampered and satisfied on every level when leaving the salon. Sometimes, a woman only has the time and energy to make one stop in her day and that stop had to be "RQ Hair Care Salon."

As soon as she began to remove her second shoe to give her other toes, the air and rest they so desperately desired, her cell phone jam came on playing DMX's *"Party Up" (Up in Here)*. She always let the song play a little before answering to a tinge of the lyrics, *"y'all gon' make me lose my mind, up in here, up in here."* It always calmed her spirits hearing DMX's raspy voice before hearing whatever her son had to share for the day's drama.

Raquel braced herself and reluctantly answered the phone. "What's up, Pook?"

"Mama, I know you at work," he started, "and at this point... sitting down resting yo' feet, but I need you to come down to the courthouse," he explained with desperation. Raquel straightened up in her seat, knowing that her moment of relaxation was on hold for a moment.

"Pook, you know I told you about working at that club and hanging around those thuggins," she retorted. She placed the phone on speaker to avoid getting a cramp in her arm with the onset of stress. Gradually, she pulled her body up out of the chair and proceeded to her office for privacy.

"Mama, I don't need this right now! You know this is a part of my job." Charles spat back in frustration. "I'm down at the Alameda County Superior Court and I go before the judge at 2pm."

"Charles Simmons, I have a head at 2pm and Jenise is one of my best clients," she paused as she felt her blood pressure rising. "Look baby, you are a grown ass man. You don't need me down there." She was beginning to think that he was not as grown as his age claimed him to be.

Charles was becoming more agitated, as he always did when things didn't go his way. "If I didn't need you," he tried to select his words carefully, "I wouldn't have called you. It will look better for me if you are here. You can be a character witness if they request it...Mama, you hear me?" She just let him ramble. "Mama?" There was nothing on her line but heavy breathing. The disregard on the part of his mother caused him to slip up. "You give them damn clients of yours more attention than you do me! We all we got!"

She took a deep breath before going in on him. "Boy, let me remind you that I am your mama and I will whoop your ass and have them lock you up for real if you ever speak crazy to me like that! Now I will see what I can do, but I *ain't* making any promises." She hung up the phone and pressed her head against the chair, contemplating whether she should jump at the request of her disadvantaged son as she often did when he found himself in a predicament.

Raquel knew it was her fault. She raised him to depend on her. Since his daddy wasn't around, she pounded into his conscience that it was just the two of them—that's it. He was a self-sufficient man in his own right, but he had trouble making any big moves without her approval, without her by his side to provide endorsement. He was her baby boy, her only boy.

Raquel pulled up to the courthouse in her 2008 Black Lexus ES 350 promptly at 1:45pm; luckily, she was able to shuffle a few clients around to reschedule Jenise and Miss Juanita. They were some of her best clients; they tipped well and rarely complained. She was very particular about being professional in business, so when Raquel had to make any adjustments in scheduling, her clients knew it had to be something important.

Raquel made it a point to be ready for all occasions. She was due to pick up her dry-cleaning from Larry's; she dashed over and picked up her gray two-piece hug-every-curve-of-her-body business suit. She then touched up her hair and make-up to stay at her best and to be supportive for her son. It wouldn't hurt to turn a few heads in the process, was her philosophy. She found a close parking spot near the front entrance and strutted into the courtroom, taking the first open seat available.

"Your Honor, I am requesting this case be thrown out. There is not sufficient evidence on my client to prove that he was involved in the alleged altercation."

The lawyer that Raquel was paying to protect her son was not going to accept no for an answer. However, the way it was looking, her son may have to serve a little time in jail. *He is going to jail.* She thought to herself. His ripping and running the streets would finally catch back up to him.

Charles Simmons was no different from all the rest of the young adult men his age; the only problem with him is that he was the only one who got caught. Back in the days of her kicking Charles and his knuckle-head-friends out of her house, he managed to always come home with the police, parking tickets, suspensions, truancy tickets, vandalism fines, nothing too serious. Fortunately, Raquel dated a few officers on the force who liked to do her favors and let him off on warnings to feel the warmth of her body late at night. Any jail time he experienced was temporary, a weekend here or there with all charges dropped, but what he was facing now would be the most serious offense yet, if convicted.

"I'm sorry, Mr. Fleming, but the prosecution has footage of your client involved in a club brawl that he initiated," the judge proclaimed. Judge Frederick Price was a veteran in the courtroom and known for locking young Black men up and throwing away the key. Charles just sat, stone-faced, unsure of what the balance would hold for him. He glanced back to see if his mother had arrived. There were all types of people gathered in the courtroom, many of which were patiently awaiting their own trials. Some were just in the vicinity and decided to sit in. He scanned the room, spotted his mother in the back, and gave her a nod to acknowledge her presence. He knew she would come through. She always did. In the end, she didn't have a choice. He was there for her; she was there for him.

"Be it as it may, Your Honor, the footage is not clear and does not prove that my client, Charles Simmons, was involved as the initiator, or connected with any altercation." Mr. Michael Fleming was a few years out of law school and still a rookie in the courtroom, but he was going to have to do. Although Ms. Simmons took in a great amount of money running *RQ Hair Care Salon*, it wasn't quite enough to cover all her personal expenses and the representation of the top-notch lawyers in the Bay Area, so Mr. Rookie Fleming was going to have to do. Plus, if Charles went to jail for a while, it would take some much needed stress off of her. Worrying about if she was going to receive that phone call or see his face on the news as another young black male murdered in Oakland, is not a mother's dream, yet a legitimate fear. He had plenty of friends, but more enemies, who at any moment would love to see him killed.

Charles is what you call a Ladies Man. *"Ladies Love Cool C,"* that's what he always used to tell his mother when she warned him about all the girls he was entertaining. Charles loved having a few girls in his face at a time and they seemed to not mind at all that their time was divided. I guess because he kept them laced with the finest things. He frequently treated his ladies to spa days, bought them expensive jewelry, and made sure that their hair was always on point. After all, his mama was the *baddest* hairdresser in town and he had them all in her shop!

Charles was no young buck, though. The case in question was a result of his surprise 30th birthday party celebration at Sweets Ballroom, in downtown Oakland, where he was the bouncer and club promoter. When he wasn't doing private security for local artists who came into town, he was keeping the city live with concerts and entertainment. He invited everyone in "The Town" to come and help him celebrate this commemorative event. He made sure that he was noticeable in his all black on black tailored *Giorgio Armani* suit and satin tie, fresh cut and all black Portello *Stacy Adams*. Raquel was not ashamed to admit to all her girlfriends that her son was attractive. Blessed with smooth cocoa skin and pearly white teeth. His dimple on his left cheek when he smiled made him all the more irresistible to the ladies. She had to remind some of her friends that he was off limits; many of them alluded to having him help them get their groove back. Although he was a well-known *playa*, it didn't stop the ladies from lining up to play on his team. And she couldn't be mad at him. He got it from his mama.

Everyone was having a blast at Sweets drinking and dancing, when all of a sudden Calvin Rogers, big-time dope dealer turned business mogul, rolled in the club starting trouble. One thing Charles never did was sell dope. He tried selling weed in middle school and again in high school, but it took too much time away from the ladies, he never could tolerate the smell either; if he didn't smell like Drakkar Noir by *Guy Laroche*, he wasn't having it. Calvin Rogers was not a fan of Charles. He felt a man of her son's caliber should be a part of his hustle, his team. Ultimately, he wanted her little baby to be his bodyguard as a part of the "Neighborhood Kings" to run all the daily security operations and make some real money, not the *Kibbles 'n Bits* he was earning from his various side jobs.

Calvin, informed that everybody in town would be at this particular party, made his presence known; he didn't have to worry about being on a guest list because he owned the majority of the nightclubs and restaurants in the city. His entrance into the event was guaranteed. He bought Charles the most expensive bottle of liquor that Sweets offered with a note attached:

*Happy Birthday C Smooth! Consider this the last time I make you an offer. Enjoy. Take it to the head!*

*C. Rogers*

He sent the bottle to the VIP section where Charles and all his homeboys and special ladies were seated. Lance immediately spotted the exchange and intercepted the bottle and the note. He knew that his boy Charles was too drunk to keep his temper from flaring up. Lance and Charles had been boys since they were in elementary school, playing baseball at the neighborhood park. He was slightly younger than Charles, but they kept a tight-knit bond like brothers. Lance always made sure to look out for his boy. If Charles was fighting, Lance was fighting, too. As a mother, if Raquel could trust anyone to look out for her son, it was Lance.

Lance slowly motioned toward Calvin to meet him by the side of the velvet rope by their VIP section and signaled to his hip where he flashed his .40 Smith & Wesson, to let Mr. Rogers know that if he was there to start trouble, it wouldn't be a beautiful day in the neighborhood. Calvin Rogers was not one to be intimidated. He took this as an immediate threat and quickly went in his coat for his .45 ACP; he shoved the 250lb security guard to the side and came straight toward Lance with the gun pointed straight in his direction. The deejay stopped the music, and all attention was on the two men. All the tipsy scantily dressed women with their five-pound weaves made every effort to maintain their composure through the pushing and shoving. One glimpse of the pistol sent all the club goers into a frenzy screaming and scattering through the nightclub, knocking over drinks and chairs as to dodge any blows or worse, a bullet.

Chairs were hurled through the air from every direction. Security created a human barricade like the Great Wall of China for the safety of those in close proximity to the commotion. The security guard quickly knocked the gun from Calvin's hand and it slid to the floor. The only logical move for any man to do in this scenario was to go to blows, and that is how the brawl started. Calvin managed to ease his way out of the club before the lights came up; he had plenty of backup to handle his dirty work. Charles remained oblivious to the whole situation; unaware that a fight had broken out on his behalf; he was engulfed in his private birthday festivities featuring a young petite sister that became his main attraction. Her conversation was not nearly as enticing as her body language. She stood about 5'9" in her red, form-fitting tube-top dress and four-inch heels with the strap exposing her French tip pedicure. None of which Charles noticed, considering he was wrapped up in conversation about him showing her his birthday suit, to accompany her birthday sex. However, Raquel kept Charles from exposing to her the details of where that ended.

Once the lights came up, the party was definitely over. Everyone made his or her move toward the door. The police were called and everyone scattered. It was Charles' party and his guests, so he was held responsible. Not to mention the fact that Lance was in possession of his unregistered gun.

"You're looking at ten years for two counts of assault, reckless endangerment and gun possession." The judge mocked, reminding him of what the chargers were against him.

As the judge spoke, several thoughts ran through Raquel's head. *One thing a mother should always have is loyalty to her family. Even when they make mistakes and do wrong, it was clearly not his fault. I always make sure that he suffers the consequences of his actions. I just can't leave that up to the justice system. Not in America. They will eat my son alive. True, I have made jokes and said that he may be better off, but what kind of mother would I be to leave my son out to dry? I didn't come all the way down to this courthouse for nothing.* Immediately she interjected, "Your honor, my son was responsible for nothing less than having a night out with friends. I can guarantee that my son had no part in this situation. As a matter of fact, at the time of the brawl, he got a call from his dad and was talking to him in the alley. I have a written affidavit from him to prove it. Not to mention, his father is on his way here to give his testimony." When all else fails, lie and have an alibi.

# Chapter 3

L ance slowly pulled up to the old-fashioned, yellow, two-story house of his childhood. It stood nestled in the cul-de-sac on the block, bumping his speaker system as loud as he could stand, broadcasting to the neighbors of his arrival. It was 6:15pm, and the sun was already beginning to descend on the day. He checked his face in the mirror to make sure his full freshly lined goatee was on point and to ensure that he didn't have any un-welcomed eye crud. Lance always made sure he was well groomed; the ladies in his life would have it no other way. He was your typical masculine man, but he knew how to dress the part for any occasion. He was a fashion connoisseur in his own right. He placed the car in park and noticed one of his three cell phones was vibrating in the passenger seat. Recognizing Charles' number on the screen, he quickly answered before it went to voicemail.

"Yo, my boy, how did court go?" Lance pressed Charles over the phone. He pulled out his house key, walked into his mama's house and threw his coat and bag on the plastic-covered couch in ritual.

"You wouldn't believe what happened, man…" Charles began, quickly interrupted by the sounds of Miss Lydia in the background.

"Is that you, son?" his mama called out to him. Lance made his way into the aroma-filled kitchen. "Get off that phone walking in my house; you know I don't play that!" Lydia slapped her son across the back of his head playfully as he kissed her on her cheek. Lydia Brown made it a point to schedule a weekly dinner with her one-and-only son. It was their special time together. She knew between all the women her son ran between, none of them knew how to take care of him. Plus, she was out of touch with men in her age bracket, so she settled for mother-and-son-date-night to keep her life exciting. The only hearty meal he would eat was through her kitchen. She felt the only way for him to maintain his 6'0" 220lb muscular frame was to nourish him with Louisiana, Southern home-style cooking, which she knew the hood rats had no clue how to conjure up.

"That's Moms. You know how that goes, don't want to get her all worked up. I will get at you later! One!" Lance immediately hung up the phone, knowing his mom didn't play, plus he knew she was cooking his favorite meal: succulent fried chicken, ox tails and gravy, golden-brown baked macaroni and cheese, okra, corn, and tomato medley and sizzling hot water cornbread. Lydia had a tendency of going overboard when it came to her son, as if she was in competition with the women he dated. There was no way in hell he was going to jeopardize a home-cooked meal. None of the females that he frequently entertained could hold a knife to his mom's cooking. As a matter-of-fact, they didn't even cook at all. He spent the majority of his TSA cash taking them out to expensive restaurants and buffets.

"Lance, baby, what's going on with Charles? Is everything okay?" Lydia questioned, concerned about her son's childhood friend after he ended his call. She overheard him mention Chuck and knew he had been previously involved in some altercation through the grapevine.

"Everything is good, Mama. I'm good; he's good, we're all good. Don't trip," he joked as he picked off a piece of the cornbread and shoved it into his mouth before his mama could snatch it out of his hand or it burned his fingertips.

"You ain't gonna want to eat yo' dinner! And your hands are dirty, Boy!" she scolded, covering the cornbread, swatting again in his direction.

"What am I? Five? I am a grown ass man, and believe me, I will eat all my dinner!" he responded, patting his chest. "I got this!"

"Boy please, sit yo' tail down! I need to talk to you." Whenever she mentioned needing to talk, he braced himself, knowing she was going to dive nose deep into his business. It was probably the reason for the Thanksgiving meal she prepared. "Now, there is this beautiful, really nice young lady I met a few weeks back, and she came into the bank today," she started without fail.

"No, Mama…nah! Hell nah!" he demanded, shaking his head and hand in unison. He knew exactly where his mama was going with the conversation and this was his attempt to stop her in her tracks before she got too deep into his life. "Mama, I got *hoes*, bad *broads, tricks and chicks,* you name it. I don't need no nice lady, you trippin." Sometimes he forgot to whom he was speaking and blurted out to her as if she were one of his homeboys. As soon as the words parted his lips, he regretted it.

"Let me remind you that I am yo' mama and not one of them raggedy street boogers you run around town with. You better respect me in my house." She popped him playfully on his hand, but topped it off with her *you are not too old to get your butt whooped* face and continued with her original statement. She believed the adage *I brought you into this world; I can surely take you out.* "Now I don't care for these 'heifers' that you are running around town entertaining. This woman is extremely beautiful, professional and I think she would be a great catch for you and an awesome mother for my grand babies!" She paused from draining the drippings from the chicken to look her son square in the face. "You are not getting any younger and I am steadily getting older and this house is empty. I could use a few crying babies to attend to."

"Check this mama; you know I got Darnise, you remember her?" Lydia looked down in anguish at the mention of the girl's name. "She is playing the role of my main chick right now, and I'm not sure if I'm ready for her to give up her starting position. She is a *baaaddd* one, and she knows how to make a *brotha feeeel gooooood.*" He closed his eyes and licked his lips, thinking back to last night.

"Boy!" she shot him a quick glance, started in his direction with the hot grease in her hand and popped him again, this time more forcefully. Lydia was not impressed with Darnise one bit. She did not respect her as a young lady. The fact that her legs were open to any and every beck and call of her son outside of a married relationship turned her stomach.

"Mama, Mama, Mama, you know I am playing. Look, I ain't no good dude. It's my own fault. I like dem *ho's,*" he pleaded in his best rendition of Lil Jon. "This girl probably goes to church, has a good job, and is looking to settle down, right? And she is probably a virgin, knowing you?" he asked inquisitively.

Lydia pulled out a chair and rested her plump body down

next to her son to rest her partially swollen feet and get more intimate for him to understand the severity of her quest. "I believe this girl will be the one to turn things around for you. I feel it in my spirit. She is a teacher at Third Street Elementary, so she definitely has that maternal instinct. She comes into Bank of America at least once a month, so she can handle her finances. She won't need your measly handouts." She took a breath and waited a brief moment before continuing. "I want the best for you, and yes, she goes to church and you know you need some Jesus! A single, young girl like her is hard to find." The last thing that Lydia desired for her son was to be anything like his father, the man who walked out of her life when he was only five years old. She made her fair share of mistakes, allowing herself to love men who failed to return the same affection. It was her mission to see to it that he didn't do the same to another woman.

Lance lifted his hand to rest on his mama's chocolate brown chin, which at this point was a bit moist from all of her slaving over the hot stove. "I hear you, mama, but I'm good! Now I'm hungry as hell...I mean heaven and I am ready to eat." It was far more difficult for him as an adult to focus and listen to her motherly wit. He knew deep down that she was right, but he wasn't ready to throw in his player card. Life was *too* good.

A thunderous banging jilted them out of their conversation. Not two seconds later, there was a loud thud against the door, like a ton of bricks landed on the front porch. The banging continued as if the entire Oakland swat team was outside of his mother's house ready to complete a drug raid.

"Lance, I know you are in there. I see yo' car outside. Open this damn door!" The banging continued, becoming louder and more violent. Lydia didn't budge, just gave him her, *I don't want to deal with this mess today* face and motioned for him to take care of the situation, before she had to go outside and handle it herself like she had to do as a teen when she and her girlfriends had problems with the jealous girls in the neighborhood. Lydia was all too familiar with Lance and his run-ins with his women. He had his car keyed, towed, windows busted and tires flattened and two out of the four incidents were at the hands of Darnise, and her ghetto cousins.

The one thing that Lydia couldn't stand more was the nasty, stank-attitude girls that her son seemed to attract. It never failed; once one of his side chicks learned about Darnise or vice-versa, they made it their mission to make his life miserable. And each and every time, Lance gave them his infamous *"I'm a man and I am not ready to settle down yet, take me or leave me speech,"* they maintained their position—on the side with no hope of promotion. He prided himself on how he was able to string women along. His boys often joked with him about being the real-life version of Bill Bellamy in *How to Be a Player*.

Lance quickly tiptoed to the door, trying not to make too much noise, looked through the peephole to see who was disturbing his dinner-date with his mama. He already knew from the loud banging just whom it was, however he needed to take extra precaution if she happened to bring back up this time as she often did.

"Lance, I'm sorry! I made a mistake. I want you back! I don't mind giving you the time you need. Just open the door and hear me out!" She peered through the window in search of a response still banging on the security gate. The voice became restless and desperate, the anger seemed to transfigure into distress. Lance waited a moment before cracking the door open. He held the door slightly ajar with one foot in his fresh

25

Jordans, ensuring that if she tried to bust the door down, she would not have any luck. The space between the wall and the door was still not wide enough for him to make out the physique of the distraught woman. He pulled the door back a little farther, enough to stick his head out and check out the scene. To his surprise, it was not who he imagined it to be.

The somewhat slender, caramel complexioned woman was perched down on the steps with her head buried in her lap sobbing profusely. Lance was a player type of guy and tried his hardest to keep the ladies from disturbing his cool, but he was definitely a sucker for tears. He believed a woman should never have to cry out of relational pain, especially on the account of him. Seeing that the coast was clear of any ambush attack, he opened the door and stepped out to console her.

"Look baby girl, don't cry. You know I hate to see you like this…but I told you not to come by here. We are not together like that. What the hell is wrong with you?" Lance checked his surroundings once more; he was raised in the hood so he was watchful for anything and everything. He inched closer to her, kneeled down, and placed his hand on her back. He began rubbing in a circular motion. The woman remained still, and she continued to weep with her face shielded by her thighs. She gradually lifted her head, wiping the tears and smudged make-up on the sleeve of her powder pink sweater. She pulled a tissue out of her Louis Vuitton purse with a faint whimper, dabbing her tears to avoid smearing her make-up any further.

"I don't know why I let you do this to me?" she managed to choke out between sobs. "All I want to do is love you and you treat me like I ain't been down for you. I do everything for you. Anything you need, I get it and give it." Her demeanor slowly began to change as she reflected on her words and what

26

once was sorrow swiftly transformed into anger yet again. She hopped up in a reverse pin drop spin and landed her open palm right on his left cheek. She switched up her arm and, with a balled fist, clocked him upside his head with her left. Immediately, she began throwing punches, landing each pound on his neck and back, any part of his body she could connect. With every blow, she spat expletives, driving her pain into his back. She kicked, scratched as he protected his face with his arms.

Lance was not in the business of putting his hands on a woman, but he was a true believer in self-defense and restraint. "Bitch, get yo' hands off me." He violently grabbed her by her slender fragile wrists, flung her around one time, stifling her attack, and slowly shook her to the ground. Her legs dangled off the side of the porch as she attempted with all of her might to squirm herself free. He wiped the sweat from his brow and let it soak into her tightly fit jeans. Although she was definitely not at her best at this moment, it was difficult for him to resist touching and skimming over her curvaceous body.

"Let me go! I'm pregnant!" she screamed at the top of her lungs as if she were trying to announce their dirty laundry to the entire neighborhood. "I came here to tell you, I'm pregnant."

Lance swiftly loosened his grip and freed her from his grasp. "What did you say?" He questioned in a panic, panting to catch his breath. "You said you were on the pill. I made sure to pull out. There is no way you are pregnant." He stared in her direction, awaiting any type of response, shaking his head in disagreement.

"Lance, I'm pregnant. I found out today. It is yours. What are you going to do about it? You said you loved me, so I stopped taking it a while ago." She cocked her head to the side like a parrot awaiting the next words to mimic. No response. She waited a moment and gradually picked herself off the ground, wiping her forehead-sweat from the tussle, trying to gain her composure. She twisted her arm, placing it on her hip, propping up her fragile body to hear how her newly informed baby daddy was going to support this new situation.

Lance remained quiet as he pondered her words. He reflected on the timeline of their last sexual encounter. He was sure that her accusation could not be true. He had no clue how he let a female jump-off get him so rattled and caught up in the *Love and Hip-Hop* drama. His mama warned him about this day. All he could hear were her words replaying in his head *these "hoochie mamas" are trouble; one night of passion can lead to a lifetime of pain.* He didn't have the courage to put his pride to the side and comfort the girl or even acknowledge her question.

"Where the hell are you going? I am talking to you?" she screamed. He turned his back on her, turned the knob of the wooden front door, and went back into the contentment and protection of his mama's house. Just before he had his entire body clear out of her sight, he stepped back and turned to her, "If what you are saying is true, you can't keep it. I'll give you the money to do what you have to do." He continued in the door and slammed it behind him.

"Do what I gotta do? Is this how you want it, Lance? You're just gonna walk away? Typical!" She bellowed in her final attempt to make peace with her now distant lover. "It's not over. Believe that! I'm keeping this baby. I'm the wrong one! But, I got something fo' that ass!" Her voice was now fading as she made her way back to her 2005 white Nissan Maxima, slamming the car door to prove her dissatisfaction with his reaction and skirted off down the street.

Lydia quickly ran back to the kitchen before Lance entered, pretending to wash the dishes as to not make it entirely obvious that she witnessed the whole ordeal. She lingered a moment before speaking, "I know I asked for grand babies, but good Lord Jesus, I didn't want them to come like this," his mother joked as she sauntered back into her chair. She had jokes too. Maybe this situation would show him just how much he needed to settle down. "If that girl is telling the truth, you know you have to do what's right, son. I know I haven't been the best example for you, but you know what it is like to not have a father around. Do you really want that for your own child?" she pleaded. "I've lived without a daddy, and the cycle has to stop. I didn't raise you like that!" Her emotions begin to take flight. The thought of her son being so disconnected from a woman that he would insinuate for her to have an abortion sent an uncomfortable charge through her body.

"That trick ain't pregnant. Even if she is, it ain't mine, Mama, believe that! There is no possible way. That's it. I don't want to talk about it anymore." He slammed his hand down on the table to seal the deal.

"How can you be so sure? And this is *my* house; I will let you know when we are finished discussing. You 'bout clear done lost yo' mind up in here."

"Mama, I'm sorry. I know that girl is up to no good. I'm positive the baby, if there is even a baby, is not mine."

She felt an edge of sincerity coming from within him. He was her heart and to see him troubled only worried her more. It had been the sole reason she felt the need to hook him up with a woman that would not try to trap him into a relationship or use him for the little money he had. It was bad enough her relationships went sour and left them in shambles, picking up all the pieces of a broken home, trying her best to make do.

"Well then, eat your food before it gets cold," his mama reminded. Making an effort to salvage what was left of their meal. She didn't want him to get any more worked up, because it was a task, calming him down.

Lance took one bite of his now cold chicken breast and threw it down, pushing the plate away. He no longer had an appetite. He had too many thoughts racing through his head. *Pregnant? She can't be.* He excused himself from the table and went back out on the front porch. He needed to clear his head. The only thing to do was to call up his boys to meet up for a drink. Although Charles had his own drama to deal with, he knew he needed to hear this. Lance scrolled down his phone to call his boy Elijah to come and swoop him up from his mama's crib. He planned to get all the way wasted and didn't want to risk driving intoxicated.

"Yo Elijah, I need you to come and swoop me." He hung up the phone, posted on the porch, and waited.

# Chapter 4

"I can still smell the liquor on your breath, honey." Charlene turned in disappointment from her husband when he tried to kiss her on her freshly painted lips. Edmond, tired from the long drive, wanted to keep the peace with his wife before exiting the car to retire to bed. It was a long trip back from Southern California and both were exhausted from all the driving and moving. Hauling boxes, bins, bags and more boxes from the truck to the dorm took its toll.

He picked up a few beers on the last leg of the trip to stay focused and alert for the duration of the drive, since Charlene would be of no assistance behind the wheel. The liquor on the drive down kept him focused enough to drown out the commentary from his wife, so he thought it best to duplicate the same ritual on the return trip. Charlene hated when Edmond drank because he became more irate and irritable with her. She was well aware of the fact that he despised her long talks and complaints about patients and co-workers in the hospital. He also couldn't stand the disdain she had with their son. However, she felt as her husband, he was obligated to be a listening ear. She had given up many of her friends to pursue her relationship with him, so it was the least he could do.

Charlene spent three days out of the week laboring twelve-hour shifts at Kaiser as a Registered Nurse. Her husband made enough money for the both of them, yet she only worked when she was tired of being alone in the house and wanted to gain some excitement in her life. Seeing open wounds and hearing crying babies invigorated her. It gave her purpose outside of her wifely duties. She had always aspired to be a nurse and help people in need. When they met at Merritt Community College, Edmond was one of her biggest supporters, encouraging her to continue when she wanted to give up and helping her out with books, when financial aid didn't quite cover everything. He was her support system, and she attempted to be his. In college, when he had his many breakdowns and blow-ups, he turned more and more to liquor. She would be the first to admit that he was no alcoholic, but she feared that one day he would take one drink too many and he would be clear on the road of no return.

The sun was beginning to set on the day, notifying them it was well past the time needed to recoup the hours sacrificed in transitioning their daughter into the real world. They managed to park the car fully in the garage this time, since the majority of the boxes Debra had packed for weeks were removed. It contained an air of emptiness with her gone, but it allowed for new opportunities in the usage of space.

"Look, honey, I don't want to fuss and fight tonight. I am tired. It was a long drive. Just give me a kiss so we can go into the house." Edmond leaned closer in hopes that she would meet him halfway and plant a luscious kiss with her full lips on his, and he could go on his merry way into the house. However, that was not the case. Charlene merely stared back in his direction. She folded her arms and repositioned her body, touching the passenger side door, propping her back against the window to gain a better view of his facial expression for her next question.

"You have been drinking a lot more lately. Is everything all right? You know you drink when you are stressed." Edmond lifted his eyes toward her, peering directly into hers. He stayed a moment and then leaned back in the opposite direction toward his door. She held her stance with her arms folded, refusing to allow him to avoid her line of questioning this time.

"I don't want to talk about it. I just want to go in my house and lay my head down on my comfortable bed." He picked up his empty beer cans and let himself out of the car, slamming the door behind him in protest of his wife's refusal of her responsibility of affection as his wife.

"Fine! I know you are just going to go to the backhouse and drink your troubles away." It was no use at all. She was speaking to the wind.

Edmond fumbled around in his pocket to locate his key. His coordination was a tad bit off, because the last ingested beer was beginning to take effect. As soon as he located the key in the midst of coins and lint in his pants pocket, he noticed the door was slightly ajar. He cautiously pushed the door in, checking around the first corner to ensure that no one had broken into their home. He grabbed the metal bat tucked away in the crevice of the wall by the entrance, for times such as this. His pistol was upstairs in their bedroom, so he settled for what was nearest. He was not alarmed. The setting read all too familiar of Samson's negligence, but it didn't hurt to take extra precaution, plus he had been drinking, causing his reflexes to be delayed. He often accidentally left doors open or unlocked, as if he could afford the coverage if any of their items were damaged or stolen. The lights were all out, but you could hear sounds of heavy breathing and moaning.

Edmond was careful with each step, maneuvering through each room, following the sounds, pretending to be *MacGyver*. As he came closer to the living room, the voice he recognized to be Samson's, along with the faint sound of a young woman. From the raucous, he initially heard when he entered the house to the faint pants; they were winding down from their private party.

"Are you sure your parents won't be back for a while?" The young girl whispered, hoping that any unwanted guests would not view their rendezvous.

"Shhh...don't talk. I'm almost finished." Samson covered her mouth with his palm, hoping she would silence her commentary in order for him to finish the task at hand. With his last pump, he raised his eyes to meet the bright light and the perturbed expression of his father. He instantly grabbed his boxers to cover his erect genitalia and slithered into them as if his life depended on it.

"Samson! What the hell is going on?" he hesitated a moment to gather his words staggering back. "Who is this floozy in my house?" Edmond didn't wait for a response. He charged at him with all the strength he could muster, lifted him to his feet by his neck, and slammed his back against the wall with each word. He tightened his grip around his neck. His heart was beating a mile a minute as sweat gathered on his forehead. He was beyond livid, and the alcohol in his system was not helping to defuse the situation. Samson squirmed within the grip, wriggling around, hoping to discover an outlet from his chokehold. His complexion turned from a dark brown to a dulling gray as he was losing air to breathe. "I told you about bringing these hoes into my house, where we lay our head. If you want to treat this house like the motel, then you need to take your ass out and pay for one like a man with integrity."

The entire ordeal caught Samson off guard. He and his father had their fair share of disagreements, but never to the extent that he felt the need to put his hands on him. He was utterly shocked that his father was so enraged that he would go as far as to attack him. "Dad, let me go! I can't breathe."

"Put him down! Edmond, get your hands off my son!" Charlene charged after Edmond, pulling at his shoulder in every attempt to free her son. "Let him go! He said he couldn't breathe." Between words, she tugged and pulled, hit, pushed her way to free her son. She managed to pry one hand from her son's neck, allowing some of his coloring to return and air back through his lungs. "What has gotten into you?" she screamed. The sound of him choking and gasping for his newly found air echoed around the living room. Charlene could not bear to watch her husband attack her son. Without realizing, he swung back in her direction, stifling her interference with his moment of discipline.

"Dammit woman! Let me handle this. He is a man, and I am handling it! I am not going to tell you again." He loosened his grip a bit to appease his wife, but he still needed Samson to understand he meant business.

"Dad…I'm sorry. Let me go!" He mustered out with limited breathing capacity.

"What is this about, Edmond? He is only doing what he has learned from you. You haven't been the best example for the boy." Charlene knew she had gone too far, but it was too late to turn back now. Her words were already deep in his subconscious. She stood suspended a moment, anticipating

35

any sudden movement. If he was drunk enough to attack his own son, he may have lost all of his good known common sense and come after her, so she braced herself.

Edmond gently released his grip and lowered Samson down to the ground. He didn't want to kill his son, but he did want to scare him enough to want to leave. Upon release, Samson scurried over to his companion to comfort her. The girl's integrity was unsheltered in her bra and panties. She lay curled up in a ball sobbing, humiliated that she allowed herself to, yet again, let another man persuade her that her value was between her legs.

"Get this girl out of my house and get out of my sight!" Samson did not waste any time making his exit. He picked up each article of clothing that lay scattered about the living room, and he and his companion made their escape. Edmond turned to give Charlene his undivided attention. "What the hell did you say to me? I really want you to say it again now that I am listening, and you have my full attention." He was panting and sweating all over his body. The sweat from his son, along with his own, soaked into his Burberry light blue cashmere sweater.

"Edmond... You heard what I said. You want to run around here like your shit don't stank, like you ain't made some bad decisions, like your ass ain't been bare-bottom in this house... caught up!" Charlene was almost in his face now. She was livid. "I don't give you any mess about it either, but count this the last time you ever put your hands on my son. Chew on this Edmond.... I am leaving. I can't do this anymore." She turned and stormed out of the room, avoiding any further eye contact. She could feel her blood pressure at its max and did not want to cause too much of a scene and end up paying for it later in the hospital. Edmond had a way of drawing her back in through his eyes. She loved him so deeply; she needed time to process her words, her disappointment. Up until this point, she had not been this vocal with him. She often swallowed her words to pacify her husband. Things were better that way; she could better deal when he was untroubled, when the seas of their life were mellow.

"Go ahead and go." Edmond raised his hand to rub his forehead and held it there in disbelief that he allowed this to go that far. He didn't want her to believe that she could just say whatever she wanted to him at any given time. He created a structured home of respect. Her first priority was to be a support to him and ensure that if nothing more, he was satisfied. He didn't abuse his wife physically in any way because she knew her place. She rarely stepped out of line. And even in times when she came very close to the line, he could give her a look that she knew she had gone too far and retreated back to her docile, submissive self.

Charlene didn't need his permission, nor was she asking for it at this point. Her words were clear, and for her; it sealed the deal of her inner thoughts. She was partway out the door once the word left her lips. She was definitely not throwing away their twenty-year marriage in any shape or form. It was time, though, for Edmond to have some think time, to understand that his family was not his enemy. She prepared a simple overnight bag and called for a taxi to come and pick her up. She didn't want Edmond to know where she was going and use the tracking device installed in her car to identify her location.

\* \* \*

"Now you know you didn't get this from me," Elijah stated matter-of-factly. The two agreed to meet in a discreet location behind the abandoned emporium outlet store in the alley to handle the transaction. It was late in the evening, so the majority of people who occupied the streets during the daylight had long gone home, leaving the night to the streetwalkers and drug dealers. One of Samson's boys gave him Elijah's contact info as the one to go to for a good price on quality guns.

"I know. I know. I won't say nothing. I'm just glad to finally have some heat. My boys have been riding me about being out in these streets with no protection." He glanced over the .45 pistol in awe that it was finally in his hands. He could hold it and it belonged to him. All his hustling paid off, and his status was now complete. "No one knows I am here, and they definitely won't know you sold it to me, believe that," Samson, still admiring the gun, responded without making eye contact.

"Good. I'm not about killin' folk, but it ain't safe in these streets without it. You a young dude and I see you out here tryin' to make yo' money. Just be careful. Everybody don't like what they see. Now, it's already locked and loaded, so you are good." Elijah wrapped it up for him and counted all the money to ensure it was there. When it came to business, he was very particular about his money, regardless if he knew you or not. "Make sure you don't tell yo' pops about this, either. I don't want him comin' after me," he joked, but serious at the same time.

"Mr. Tucker is the last person who I would tell about this. I'm not at the house right now anyway because he kicked me out." Samson kept his eyes on the concealed gun, excited that he was finally in the game. He could not wait to get back to his boys to show off his new toy and security system. If his dad happened to find out, it would not be through him.

"Word? What happened?" Elijah requested.

"I got caught up with one of my ladies. Pops came home from Riverside and walked in on us gettin' it in, in the living room. He was drunk, flipped out, and kicked me out of the house. So now I really need that heat, if I'ma be out here in these streets." Samson responded with almost an air of arrogance. In his mind, this was his opportunity to finally be the man he was living in his head.

As Elijah was wrapping up their transaction, a call came through on his Blackberry. "What's up, L Boogie? Give me a minute, I am finishing up some business and I'll be right there to swoop you up." He hung up the phone and parted ways with Samson dipping through the alley without a beat.

The nightfall's fifty-degree weather began to settle in. Samson knew it was best to get back to his chick's house since he left his Nautica wool-blend pea coat that he rarely left home without, at his father's house in his haste to get away. As he scanned the area for crackheads or muggers lurking in the dark corners, an all-black Cadillac Escalade crept up on the side of him, catching him off guard just before the exit of the alley. Samson reached back for his backpack. Now that he had protection, he didn't hesitate to give it some exercise, especially if it meant saving his life. The driver's side window slowly descended, exposing only the eyes of the gentleman seated inside, hidden by black *Ray-Ban* sunglasses.

"No need to be alarmed, Young Blood. I'm an old friend of your father's. I saw you back there conducting some kind of business. You got to be more careful." Samson wasn't sure if this was some kind of setup or ambush orchestrated by Elijah to get him for his merchandise. It seemed highly unlikely, but when a man was in distress, he would do anything to make sure he was eating.

"I'm good. I don't need nobody lookin' out for me." Samson poked his chest out, lifting his chin as his father instructed him to show he was a man and unafraid.

"Calm down Young Blood. I'm not your enemy. As a matter-of-fact you don't even want me to be your enemy." Samson kept his stance with his eyes directly on the man engaging him. His hand stayed positioned behind his back in his bag in case he made any sudden movements. "I'll tell you what, my name is Calvin Rogers, and you seem like a good kid with your head on your shoulders." Samson waited in suspense. He knew that a proposition was coming next. He was no stranger to the streets; he heard all about Calvin Rogers. Although he had never seen him before, he definitely didn't know that his father had any dealings with him, but Calvin meant money, status, and power. If he could get all those without the help of his father, he was down to do just about anything. "How about you come and work for me? Don't think of me being your boss; I don't operate like that. This is an opportunity for you to have your own business and even have some employers working under you. How does that sound?"

*How does that sound?* Samson thought back to himself. This was an opportunity of a lifetime. Calvin Rogers was not in the habit of just offering anybody a job or accepting rejection when the offer was placed on the table. He didn't trust enough for that. He had to say yes. It could be life or death.

"Can I ask you a question?" Still holding his stance, but a bit more relaxed knowing he was in good company.

"Spit it out, Young Blood. I'm on a time schedule and I don't make it a point to be turned down." He lowered the window all the way down so his entire face was visible. He removed his sunglasses to give man-to-man eye contact.

"How do you know my father? And how did you know I was his son?" Samson was not sure if he even desired to know the answer, but he felt it right to ask considering the circumstances of his situation.

Calvin laughed to himself, "Young Blood, your father and I go way back. Back before you were even born, but I will let him tell you all about that one day. Just know that I once had his back. He owes me his life. I was there for him in the greatest time of need, when no one else was. So, what do you say?" Mr. Rogers felt this was the last time he was going to place the offer on the table. It was rapidly approaching its expiration.

"I'm down." Samson remarked with no hesitation. He was convinced that if his dad owed him his life, that he could trust him to improve his. Samson saw dollar signs and instant street credibility. He would be the talk of the town amongst his boys when they found out. Not to mention, now he had his gun.

"Good. Consider yourself a King. Now I am a businessman, and I like to conduct my business in private. You can't tell anyone that you are working with me. Trust, people will know soon enough, but not by the way of your mouth. You understand Young Blood?"

"Understood," he replied, to prove he accepted the agreement. Samson was well aware of the conditions of his partnership with Mr. Rogers. Part of him knew that what he was embarking on would upset his father. And in many ways, it was his form of revenge. If his father truly wanted him to be out of his house, he was left with no other choice but to survive on his own.

41

"Hop in the car. We are going to go for a ride." Calvin Rogers instructed his driver to open the door for Samson and he crawled in, awaiting his rite of passage into manhood.

# Chapter 5

The Shadow Bar was abnormally packed on this particular night. Lance, Charles and Elijah were greeted by the hostess and escorted through, like royalty, to the private area in the rear. As a promoter and club bouncer, Charles frequented all the hot spots in town and maintained a good standing relationship with the owners. The guys located the perfect table in the club that was conducive to the serious yet revealing conversation they intended to have. The DJ was on point, spinning the hottest '90s hip-hop and R&B jams. The vibe was mellow; couples, sexy ladies, sugar daddies were all out to have a good time through vibrant conversation and stimulating libations. The guys were not fully dressed for the occasion, but their reputations around town made up for their ill-intended dress attire. The crew often frequented this particular bar due to the reasonable drink offerings and the sassy, sexy, sophisticated women that found themselves there after work for happy hours and Girls' Night Out.

After the first round of drinks was ordered, Lance interrupted the nonsense chatter. "So Bruh, how did you manage to get off?" Lance wanted to get the lowdown on the real matter of why they met up. He was still bothered by the previous encounter that unfolded at his mama's house, and any other news would help to shake his discomfort.

"Man...they couldn't prove a damn thing. Yo boy had a real good lawyer and, not to mention Pops, came down and spoke a good word on my behalf. O.G. got pull." He stated, reassured and took a sip of his beer, relieved that he was a free man.

"I don't know what yo' pops is really into, but he got a lot more going on than cars. I ain't mad at him, though. At least you are out." Elijah followed suit and took a sip of his beer. Elijah prided himself on his ability to hustle and get things done, but he had a special admiration for him. When he did things, he made it count.

Elijah was the friend in the crew that everybody could rely on. Anything and everything you needed—he either had a hook-up on it, knew where to purchase it, or how to fix it. When he received the call from Lance, he immediately stopped what he was doing to make sure that he was good. Actually, anytime any one of his boys was in a bind, he made sure to see that they were taken care of. He was almost like a big brother. He was a few years older than the rest of them. At thirty-five, he had the wisdom and street smarts of one of the triple Original Gangsters on the block in the neighborhood.

"Moms did her thang as well. Got yo boy, a lawyer and all." Charles added, smiling proudly that his mama came through as he knew she would. "I was ordered to pay a criminal fine and two times the amount of overall damages. It comes out to be about $15,000, but y'all know I can pull that in a few weeks! Plus, if I need any money, I can get it from Lance." They all laughed and bumped fists, clanged their beer bottles together and sipped in unison, toasting to another chance at life. The burden of spending unearned time in jail was not on Charles' agenda.

The young waitress assigned to their area sauntered her way over to the table and collected the empty beer bottles distributed across the table. Her low-cut Shadow V-neck t-shirt exposed just enough skin to get their attention long enough to interrupt the conversation for a moment. All three of them looked like little boys in the candy store drooling over the sugary spread. She somehow managed to always wait on the tables of the eligible bachelors that stepped foot in the nightclub and took advantage.

"Are you boys having anything else?" she asked seductively, batting her eyes slightly bent over the table to give a little cleavage surprise.

"Nah...I think we are good right now, baby girl, unless you are offering your number." Lance never missed an opportunity to add a girl to the team. She leaned into him, resting her breast on his right shoulder and whispered in his ear.

"Before you leave out of here, make sure that you come see me." She turned and walked away and put an extra twist on her walk because she knew the boys were watching like hawks. Her black mini skirt was just long enough to cover her butt cheeks, but any extra bend or gust of wind would reveal all that her mama gave her.

"Damn! Can a brotha get some love?" Elijah joked. "Don't you have enough trouble in yo' life? You trying to add another trick to the roster?"

"I can't help the fact that these hoes want me!" Lance spared them no filter. "Which reminds me, I brought y'all down here so I can clear my head." He took another sip of his beer. He peered over at Charles to see how he was holding up.

"Chuck, bruh... you good?" Lance questioned.

"Yep. I'm good. I got to get this money, but other than that, I'm straight."

"How is that chick you were hugged up with at the club on your birthday?" He kept his eyes on his expression and body language, taking another sip of his beer.

"After I hit that... I let the broad go. She was crazy. She tried to get me for my money after I fell asleep. *And* she tried to save the condom. You know I was gone that night drunk off that *Hennessy*. I normally don't let them spend the night, but I had no choice. When I woke up in the middle of the night, she was all in my wallet. Caught her ass red-handed!"

"Damn, dawg. What did you do?" Lance asked, trying to show concern for his boy.

"I threw her ass out. What you think I did? In her panties and all. She tried to play me, though. Said she was just trying to put her number in my wallet. What part of the game is that?"

Lance hesitated a moment before he spoke again. "Tanisha came by the house the other day, claiming I got her pregnant!"

"My Tanisha? What the hell?" Charles immediately rose up in his seat, thrusting toward Lance to make a move. Elijah remained seated, silent, anticipating the answer to Charles's question. He knew his friend was promiscuous; however, he didn't imagine that with all the women in the city that Lance would find himself with one of his patna's girls. "She played me behind my back, messin' with the homie?"

"Dawg. I got caught up. That chick got me! I didn't know that y'all slept together. She told me you weren't interested, and you know a brotha got a weak spot for red bones with that thickness. So, I jumped on that!" Lance responded, attempting to reason with Charles. He hoped he would understand his dilemma and offer his immediate forgiveness.

"Tanisha Watkins is crazy, and so is her family. Her brother Tony tried to roll up on me the next day. I pulled out my pistol, and he understood what time it was. But now you got to deal with her," he remarked sarcastically. "I would never put no hoe before my fam, but for *that*, I hope she *is* pregnant because that is what yo ass gets." Charles sat back in his chair, relieved that he didn't have to deal with her or her scheming tactics. Lance was his boy, but they had their fair share of fistfights, nothing too serious that would break up the brotherhood. "I got 99 problems, but *that bitch* ain't one," Charles mocked, channeling his inner Jay-Z.

"Well, it ain't no fun if all the homies can't have none," Elijah joked, to lighten the mood back up. Yet with a serious smirk on his face, as if they obliged, he would be down for the cause. "Does she have a sister?"

"I can't believe yo ass though" Charles shook his head. Honestly, very thankful that night he used protection and caught her when she ventured to steal his sperm. After that night, he threw her out; he hadn't heard from her. Charles and Lance were not in the business of discussing the women that they slept with, unless when things came up that were important: pregnancy, STDs, vandalism of any kind, regarding the women—it was cause for a man-to-man conversation.

"I'm sorry to interrupt your conversation, but is one of you, Lance Brown?" A beautiful mocha-chocolate skinned young lady dressed in black slacks and a red blazer approached the table. Her soft brown, classy bob styled hair complemented her appearance. She appeared no older than twenty-five, amiable and maternal in nature.

"It depends on who's asking, sweetheart?" Elijah sat up in his chair and put his hand down underneath the table by his hip. It wasn't out of the ordinary for gangsters to use women as a decoy to set things off in the club. With all the news he was receiving today, he was very much on edge.

"Well…my name is Jamie Lynn Johnson and I know Lance's mom, Miss Lydia. She told me I could find him here. She called me and said that we could talk because you probably really needed someone right now." Jamie was speaking, looking into the faces of all three men, not sure which one was actually Lance. The owner informed her of where they were seated at the back of the club. "I don't normally come into places like this, but she seemed so worried that I came to just make sure that all was well."

"Say no more beautiful. I am Lance." Lance turned and smiled. He considered this the perfect opportunity to escape the intense conversation. He lifted her hand and gently kissed it. "This is probably not the best place for us to have our first encounter, but since you are here, we can go somewhere and grab a bite to eat." Lance knew that there was too much commotion in the bar to have any type of meaningful conversation. He nearly neglected the fact that his boys were present; his mind was focused and ready to take her for a night out on the town.

"I think I would like that. I *am* hungry. Where should we meet?" Lance placed his hand around her waist to guide her out of the club. As he motioned to trail behind her, he remembered that he left his car back at his mama's house and Elijah had been his driver when he offered up the invitation. He was not nearly as drunk as he had planned to be. Luckily, it worked out because he was not very pleasant as a sloppy drunk. His expletives and raunchy demeanor would have immediately turned her off.

"Oh... I actually don't have my car. It is not normally my style to ask a woman to drive me around, but if you don't mind...can I ride with you?"

Jamie Lynn consented. Most of the information about Lance that she obtained was second hand through Miss Lydia, yet she still felt connected to him. She trusted her instinct with this one in hopes that maybe he truly was "the one" for her. Lydia often shared stories and tales about her son and the many women that corrupted his potential, ensuring her that she did not raise her son in that way, and all he needed was a wholesome woman to snap him back into shape. He was a good man in the rough.

Lance turned and clutched his beer bottle, savoring the last sip of his beverage and communicated to his boys he would catch up with them later with a few hand gestures. Charles, still a bit disappointed in his friend, just shook his head. Although they were close, he knew the type of man Lance was and the misleading lifestyle he led. Charles was a ladies' man as well, yet he avoided leading any woman to believe that it was any more than what it was. He steered clear of long-term relationships or commitment. He was not a fan of monogamy and made it very clear to all the women he entertained. To Charles, this girl seemed different; really sweet and innocent, too good for Lance.

"That dude stays getting women. He already got that one ho' pregnant and now he is leaving with *that* fine ass woman? I ain't no hater. I'm just saying," pointing in their direction, Charles whispered under his breath to Elijah as Lance was exiting the table.

"There is no way he is going to keep playing with fire and not get burned." Elijah paused and looked at his half empty beer bottle. "At least, that is what my mama always told me." They both laughed at his maternal wisdom and kept drinking.

The waitress noticed Lance leaving the club with Jamie Lynn and marched over to him before he reached the entrance door. She slid her black pump in the aisleway, blocking them from exiting, dug her freshly polished, red fingernails into her cleavage, pulling out a crumpled piece of a bar napkin with her number affixed on it. She gently pressed it into his hands as a reminder that she didn't forget about him. Jamie's presence had no effect on her plan. She paid her no mind, leaned into him again, and whispered into his ear. *"Make sure you use it."* To seal the deal, she gently stuck her tongue in his ear and swirled it around. Taking a slurp of his earlobe, she finally released it with her teeth. "Don't keep me waiting." She cut her eyes back at Jamie, scanning her up and down, dumbfounded as to why he was leaving the club with her instead.

Jamie Lynn pushed past the scarlet woman, jetting out to her car that was parked directly across the street. "I don't have time to deal with thirsty women. I definitely didn't come out here to be disrespected."

Distracted by his ear action, Lance almost missed her breaking away. "Jamie, wait up." He quickly followed her out onto the sidewalk, hoping to stop her. "Wait up, please. I don't know that woman." Lance softened his tone.

"Well, it sure looked like you did." Lance reached out and grabbed her wrist. Jamie jerked back and stopped in her tracks to hear what he had to say and to avoid any further attention brought to their conversation. "Now, I am not your girl and you don't even know me at all. But I refuse to be disrespected. If that is your lady, I apologize for being in her way." She folded her arms and looked away in frustration. A few of the bar patrons who noticed the commotion observed the exchange.

"It's not like that." He took the napkin that was still in his hand, tore it into small pieces, and dropped it right on the sidewalk where they were standing. "I don't know that woman. I just met her tonight and I guess she thought she had to go above and beyond for her tip. She only did all that to make you jealous because she knows she is ugly." Lance smiled and nudged her arm, trying to make a joke out of the situation. Jamie stayed stone-faced, still awaiting his explanation why she should proceed with an evening with him. "Tell me this, Queen. Why did you come down here?" Lance used the utmost respect when he was in the company of intelligent women. In addition, he knew he was in a tight space. His mama schooled him on how to woo a lady.

"Honestly, your mother speaks so highly of you when I go into the bank. She told me you have some women's issues, but that a woman like me was what you needed. I guess I wanted to see for myself."

"Well, that is true to a certain extent, but please understand that if it was me and you, you would not have to worry about a thing. If you just give me an opportunity to show you what I am about, I am sure that we can get past all this." He took a step closer to her and placed his hand on the side of her face, gently caressing it. His hand was almost covering the entire side of her cheek. He slid his palm down and rested his fingertips on her chin. He flashed a reassuring smile. "Will you allow me to take you out?"

Jamie could not resist his charm. She loved a challenge. Any man that was too easy to attain was a turnoff for her. A little competition never hurt anyone, especially if she was winning in the end. She pushed the button to unlock the car and motioned for him to come onto the other side. She was still hungry and with all the recent unfolding of events; it was the least she deserved. Lance opened her door, gently protecting her head, making sure she was securely in before he ran to the passenger side and hopped in.

Jamie checked her mirrors and noticed a silver Range Rover creeping up on the side of her car, blocking her from pulling out of her parking space. The high beam lights were piercing her eyes, making it difficult to make out a clear picture of the driver. A medium-sized woman about 5'5" hopped out of the car with a wooden baseball bat in her hand. Three other women surrounded the car on all sides, yelling for Lance to exit the car and confront them. *I don't need this.* Lance thought to himself, recognizing it was Darnise and her ghetto cousins, which he often referred to as the "Zoo Crew." When it came time to get revenge on the men that so easily did her wrong, her cousins knew how to put fear in the hearts of men, take them to school and teach them that messing with family was a huge mistake. They were her ride-or-die chicks. He immediately leaped back out of the car to intersect any intentions of the perturbed women. Darnise was known to get down with the best of them in the neighborhood, fighting with no rules. Lance figured it would be utterly impossible for Jamie to take down these ruthless gutter rats on her own, especially on his behalf.

"Darnise, this is not the time or the place for this," Lance stated, trying to reason with her.

"This is how you treat me? All these years and you are blowing me off for the next…" Darnise was instantly cut off by Jamie.

"Lance, get back in the car, please." Jamie spoke firmly through the lowered passenger side window. Lance didn't seem to understand her request and stared blankly back at her as if she was speaking another language. He took another step toward Darnise with his hands raised, hoping she would surrender, allowing everyone to depart from the scene unharmed. "Get yo' ass back in the car!" She repeated, this time screaming. Lance immediately jumped back in the car at her request. The whole ordeal was turning him on. The fact that the two women were ready to go to blows in his honor boosted his ego; at least he saw it that way in his head. He secured himself in the car, she put her car in reverse, hit a quick U-turn and was out of their sight.

Charles and Elijah devoured as many beers as their stomachs could tolerate. They needed to remain functional and decided it was best that they sober up a bit to get home. The waitress brought over a couple glasses of ice water and the bill to close out the order. Charles dug deep into his handy arsenal of cheesy pickup lines and dusted off a few of the award-winning options he would plant on the waitress when she returned. He whistled to grab her attention with a few snaps, hoping that since Lance jetted out on him, he didn't need her contact information. It would be his honor as his friend to pick up the pieces. She just rolled her eyes, wiping down the table, hoping he got the message that she was not interested.

The scrolling strobe lights from the DJ booth flashed on the entrance. Charles spotted Darnise and her cousins trudging into the establishment in his direction. He lowered his head as she scanned the room in search of someone. With her crew beside her, they stuck out like a sore thumb.

Darnise kept in shape. Lance liked to describe her as "healthy in all the right places." From his perspective, milk did her body good. However, her attitude often worked as a defense toward

53

men who were interested. She was far from an ugly girl, but her cousins often overshadowed her beauty with their bright indiscreet red, pink and blue weave colors, nails and lashes. Her skin-tight black freak 'um dress pressed every single curve of her body. It was obvious to him that she had an agenda that evening that quickly faded to black. She caught the attention of all the patrons as their eyes were glued to her and her posse. She appeared to be in search of someone. She was panting, her chest inflated and deflated with each breath. He wanted to approach her, yet he knew that if Darnise was in the building just after Lance left, that the two probably had a showdown in the parking lot that Charles knew he wanted no part of. He buried his head down in his arms, hoping that she would not notice him and carry on with her evening. She was too determined for that. She made her way to the back of the bar, thoroughly glancing over each and every guest seated at their respective tables.

"Charles, I see you! Why are you acting like you don't see me in here?" Charles continued to keep his head lowered in hopes that she would think it was a mistaken identity and leave. "I knew you would be in here; I saw yo' car, so I knew Lance would not be far behind. Who is that girl that he left out of here with?"

"Oh, hey Darnise, that *is* you. I almost didn't recognize you in the dark."

"Don't play games with me, Chuck. Who is the girl Lance left here with?" Her cousins stood watch around the table, focusing on the entrance and exit doors.

"I ain't got nothing to do with y'all situation. I don't know the girl, but if you really want answers, you should go holla at Miss Lydia. I am sure she is just waiting to tell you all about it."

He smirked with a hint of sarcasm in his tone, knowing Miss Lydia wouldn't dare to entertain a conversation with her.

"Come on y'all, let's get out of here!" Darnise exclaimed, rounding up her cousins, disappointed that he was of no assistance to her. She huffed and puffed like a six-year-old girl the entire route from the table to the exit. She completely ignored the advances from the men in the bar that grabbed for her wrists to catch her before bursting out of the club.

The hour was growing late; by now, Charles ingested two beers over his public drinking limit. Elijah was alert, not nearly as intoxicated as his friend. He decided to go out and grab Charles' car from the valet. It was best for him to drive Charles home and retrieve his car the next day after he sobered up a bit. Elijah made the arrangements with the owner to leave his vehicle overnight and presented the valet with the ticket for Charles' car. The young man dashed off down the dimly lit street and returned in seconds with the vehicle.

Elijah pulled out a crisp twenty-dollar bill and handed it to the parking attendant for his marvelous work in not damaging or scratching his boy's baby. Charles' black on black fifth generation Chevy Camaro was his pride and joy. He opened the car door, turned up the CD player, rested his head on the headrest, and waited for Charles to make his way out of the bar. Without warning, the sound of Fourth of July fireworks exploded in his ear, the front windshield and passenger side windows immediately shattered, scattering small pieces of glass throughout the interior of the car.

The next sounds were more recognizable. As each round was emptied into his vehicle, his body seamlessly reacted to every impacted bullet. Blood leaked from his flesh into the fabric of the seats, covering what was left of the glass still standing. The sleek leather upholstery was tattered, exposing the underlying cushion. After the first three shots, Elijah gasped for air, gurgling, trying to fight against the influx of fluid that was entering his mouth. The next three shots delivered his unwarranted fate.

The entire body of bar patrons rushed to the front of The Shadow Bar after the ringing of shots fired ceased to witness who the unsuspecting victim would be. Charles was clear as soon as he recognized his mutilated car, now a casket holding his friend. He frantically sprinted over to the car in disbelief that something like this could happen. He searched left and right for any sign of the killer.

"Somebody call an ambulance!" he hollered to the people, who stood immobile with no urgency. "Somebody call 911!"

# Chapter 6

"Samson, let me speak to mama." I forced out with all my mustered up strength.

"She's not here. What's up?" he asked with grave concern. "You need something? Somebody messin' with you?"

"No, fool. You can't do anything anyway," I responded with irritation. "Where's Mama?"

"I told you she ain't here!" he repeated in the same manner as the first time.

Samson was a master of getting under my skin. For some reason, he thought he could fix everything for me and fight all my battles. One time back when I was in middle school, this really hideous, overweight eighth grade monster of a girl tried to punk me for my lunch. In actuality, she did punk me for my lunch, my peanut butter and jelly sandwich and goldfish. She shoved me in the middle of the cafeteria, knocking me to the ground in front of all the students. I looked up as she took a bite out of my sandwich, leaving crumbs on her lip and chin. She didn't even have the decency to wipe off her filthy mouth.

Word got back to my brother, who happened to be at school that day. Normally, he would be behind the bungalows smoking weed with his buddies or cutting school to hang out at the local barbershop. This day he waited until the final school bell rang and surrounded the big black roly-poly roach girl with his friends. He forced me to spit in her face as he knocked her to the ground. He and one of his boys held her down; he instructed me to sock her in the head and kick her in the stomach. I didn't want to look like a punk again, so I did it. I was fearful that as soon as he was no longer around to protect me, she would have me slaughtered. She would fry me up and have me for supper. But I manned up and did as I was told. From that day on, she left me alone. I knew that anytime somebody bothered me, that he would not hesitate getting involved. Yet that is what I feared, and often the boys that I had crushes on were his homeboys or his enemies, which made all of them off limits.

"Well, when Mama gets home, tell her to call me. It's an emergency," I demanded.

"I don't think that Mama is going to be home for a while," he started with some hesitation. "Mama and Daddy got into it again. They were cussin and yelling, so you know it had to be something bad, because Mama doesn't ever use that kind of language. Daddy just walked out into the back house where he keeps his liquor and never came back in. He didn't take his truck this time. I know he is back there getting drunk. Mama packed a small overnight bag and smashed out. I'm sure she went to Big Mama's, but you know I ain't mad because that means I get the house to myself," he smirked. "I think I might just call one of my shorties over to the house." He conveniently left out the truth of the matter, but I had already heard what went down.

"Boy, please! None of these girls are checking for you, unless you are about to call one of those hoodrats! You know the one Mama and Daddy caught you fooling around with when they returned from Riverside. They said she was all the way tore up, from the floor up, basket weave and all!" I reminded him through my panting. "But never mind all that; when Mama gets home, have her call me, please?"

"You right. I just stopped by the house real quick to pick up some clothes. Pops doesn't even know I am here, but if I see Mama, I'll tell her. Bet. Gone."

The dial tone revealed the harsh reality that I would have to face this alone. I tossed my cell phone to the side, slowly picking myself off the bathroom floor, trying to avoid my fresh vomit spread over the toilet seat and floor. The odor from my regurgitated breakfast, lunch or dinner, because I was definitely unsure of which one caused my insides to turn. I was empty. My stomach had no more acid to release. My lower back, abdominal pain, and headaches made it very difficult for me to keep my food down, not to mention the sight of endless blood made me nauseated. My head was spinning and pounding. Every gasp for new breath sent my body into shock. It felt like a sharp knife was driving into my belly repeatedly.

My roommate had not arrived home from work to assist me in my weakened state or to hound me with questions of my condition. Although we had just met, we had an instant connection. She was studying the same major at U.C. Riverside and came from a similar home environment. I was certain that my mother would have a-million-and-one questions to ask me as well, but at the end of the day, she was my mother and she would understand. She would be able to provide some answers for me. She could lead me in the right direction of what decision to make, and she would be able to make me feel better about myself right now.

Ha. Who was I kidding? My mother was never there for

me when I was sick, or at all, for that matter. The one time I stayed home due to severe menstrual cramping, she was too busy attending to other endeavors. This is code for cleaning up Samson's mess or preoccupied with her patients at the hospital. I had to get my own heating pad. My tears didn't sway her in any way. She claimed I was being a baby and to suck it up. "Women hurt and go through pain" she would tell me, "so get used to it now; so you can endure it later." Every opportunity provided for my mother to be just *that* was lost amidst her inability to connect with me. We were constantly at odds. Don't get me wrong. We love each other; we just didn't speak it verbally. We show it uniquely—at least that is what I came to believe and understand. To the outside world, it may be classified as dysfunction, but in our little world, it was our existence.

I knew that being alone was not the best option for me. I had to get myself to a hospital or to the Health Clinic on campus, but I didn't have a car. 9-1-1 was the only course of action. I propped myself against the cabinet with my half-naked body exposed to the icy chill from the floor. My numb fingers trembled as I juggled the phone in my hand. I was terrified.

The night prior, after much coaxing from my roommate, I surrendered and purchased an over-the-counter Early Home Pregnancy Test Kit. I knew that taking one at-home pregnancy test was not the most efficient way to determine if I was, in fact, pregnant, but I had to know. I remembered learning that there may not be enough hormones in the urine after a missed period to make that declaration.

My body just didn't feel the same, my breast were slightly larger and my nipples were sometimes numb. I shrugged it off as typical menstrual symptoms because there was no way I was pregnant after one time of meaningless sex. It was certainly not baby making or lovemaking. I despised every minute of it. Okay, let's not say I despised it, but I was not prepared or mature enough for the moment. I agreed to have sex because I refused to be the only freshman virgin in college.

I did exactly as instructed, laid the test on a flat surface, and soaked it with my urine. I waited for what felt like an eternity for the results of the test. Finally, within the small square portion of the test, my fate appeared.

"9-1-1 Karen, what's your emergency?" The voiced boomed in my ear.

"I'm not sure what is going on with me." I felt an anxiety attack sneaking up on me. "I'm alone. There's blood everywhere." I attempted to steady my breathing, but to no avail. "I can't stop vomiting." My hands were trembling, making it difficult to maintain the phone in my cold, numb fingers. "Please help! I'm scared!" My words echoed in my own ear.

"OK. What is the location of the emergency?" the operator requested.

"I'm at 3...5...9...5... Can-yon Crest Drive."

"OK. And is that a house or an apartment?"

"It's an apartment. Can you send someone, please?" The operator's lack of urgency annoyed me. I could feel the sweat from my pores soaking into my underclothes, which were already soiled with blood.

"And what's the name of the housing unit?"

"The Plaza. Unit 125." I scanned the room. My eyes focused on the door. I was hoping my roommate would come busting in the door to my rescue.

"What is the phone number you are calling from?"

"951-555-7928" With each question, I felt my temperature rising and my eyes welled with tears. I swallowed hard to keep myself from crying, inhaling, and exhaling.

"And what's your name?"

"Debra Tucker."

"And how old are you?"

"I'm seventeen."

"Is the bleeding serious? Do you feel like you may lose consciousness?"

"I've never bled like this before. Please help me! Send someone now! I can't take these pains in my stomach." The pains were becoming more severe and frequent.

"OK. We have an ambulance on the way. That is 3595 Canyon Crest Drive, correct?"

"Yes! Please hurry!"

"OK. We have help on the way. If anything changes or gets worse, please call us back at 9-1-1."

I hung up the phone and situated my head on a rolled up bathroom towel, shifting my body into the fetal position. I closed my eyes and began to pray for the Lord to make it all right. Although we didn't frequent church, we did pray at home. That's all I knew how to do. Church was never a priority in our home. My dad spent many Sundays locked away in his man cave, enjoying his day off. Big Mama often urged us to attend with her, but my mom never quite saw the need. As long as she knew how to get a prayer through, it was enough.

It took the Emergency Medical Technicians nearly five minutes to come to my rescue. The last thing I remembered was being loaded onto the stretcher. *Thank you, God!*

The bright lights pierced my eyelids, forcing them to open.

I was sprawled across the hospital bed in the private room, surrounded by all the different pieces of medical equipment. I had multiple tubes and lines branching from my limbs. The beeps, buzzes and alarms made getting any rest virtually impossible. I slowly lifted my right arm to view the arterial line that was nipping my skin. Gradually, I shifted my head to examine the line attached to the monitor to ensure my blood pressure was good. 117/76 mm Hg, my blood pressure was normal. I was fine. I wanted nothing more than to get out of that hospital bed and back to the normalcy of my apartment. *Did no one come to see if I was OK? How long have I been here? Did my mama call me back?* All these thoughts rushed through my mind. The petite Filipina registered nurse who was assigned to my room abruptly interrupted my pondering. She lightly tapped on the door to notify me of her entering the room. Her voice was sweet and soothing, almost making me feel at ease in the frigid recovery area. The pale wall coverings and unappealing pastel drapes effectively prevented the outside world from breaking its way in.

"Hi, my name is Ana and I am your nurse. I am here to take your vitals and verify if you need any additional treatments," she explained.

"Is everything OK?" I inquired with dire concern.

"Dr. White will be in shortly to explain what happened?" She carefully noted all my vitals on her chart and left me to my wondering thoughts. I decided I would attempt to rest my eyes a bit before my doctor arrived.

Just as I began to journey into the first stage of REM, my doctor entered the room, "Hello Debra. I'm Dr. White. I'm glad to see you are awake and feeling better." I was not quite awake, however I was delighted that my doctor was young,

African-American and female. That was not common where I was from; it even lifted my spirits. All the times I went to visit my mother at work, I never saw a young sista, brotha, or any Black person for that matter, as a doctor.

I still remained weak. I repositioned myself on the hardwood-floor-of-a-bed and braced myself for her report.

"Did you know you were pregnant?" She jumped right into it. For a moment, I had even forgotten the reason I was there in the first place.

"Yes." I said with hesitation.

"When did you find out?"

"Last night." I was unclear where the line of questioning was leading, but I decided to be compliant.

"So you haven't taken any prenatal vitamins?" With each question, she made notations on her clipboard.

"I'm sorry, doctor, but I don't know why you are asking me all of these questions. Is there something wrong? Is my baby okay?"

"Ms. Tucker, when the paramedics arrived at your apartment you were going in and out of consciousness, due to the fact that you were losing so much blood. You originally called because you were experiencing abdominal pain and excessive bleeding. We were able to get you stabilized and your vitals within the normal limit. We ordered some stat labs, drew blood and placed an IV in your arm to distribute fluids throughout your body." She noticed the confusion and concern in my expression and got straight to the point. "You were experiencing what is referred to as an active bleed, so we immediately transferred you up to surgery. It was a life or death situation…so we proceeded with the surgery."

"I don't follow you, doctor. What are you telling me?" I felt my body temperature rising and my palms moistened. I was feeling nauseated all over again; too much was happening too fast. I wished my father were here to scoop me up in his arms and tell me everything would be all right. He would rub my back and whisper in my ear that it was just a nightmare and all would be fine in the morning. He would offer me warm milk and chocolate chip cookies just for his precious baby girl. But I knew this was real, all too real.

"We had to conduct an emergency dilation and curettage surgery to remove all the small pieces of the placenta." My throat immediately dropped to my stomach and my breath became shortened. I began to gasp for air. The medical blanket that draped over my leg shielding my bare legs from the arctic temperature was having a reverse effect on my body. Chills ran up and down my spine, arms and legs. I was overreacting, yet I couldn't control myself. All I heard the doctor saying was breathe, breathe, breathe.

Inhale. Exhale. Inhale. Exhale. I could feel myself regaining control of my breathing. The doctor was extremely patient with me. My intuition was telling me that she could somehow relate to my situation. When I gazed back in her direction, her face told me that was not the end of her announcement.

"Based on the ultra sound you were seven weeks pregnant and typically within the first trimester spontaneous miscarriages can occur," she continued. She appeared so matter-of-fact there was no denying her conclusion. "Unfortunately, due to the procedure and your medical condition, the likeliness of you having children in the future has significantly decreased. We were unable to get in touch with your parents. Were they aware of that you were pregnant?"

It had not dawned on me until that moment that my mother

never called me back. I wanted to tell her what was going on, but she was just too busy. It was bad enough that I was unable to get a hold of her, but the hospital was unsuccessful as well. I was ashamed and embarrassed to be unaccompanied at the hospital and worse, no one cared to be by my side.

"What about the father of the baby? Was he aware of the pregnancy?"

I became so engulfed in my own thoughts that I didn't realize the doctor was still in the room awaiting my answer. Of course, he didn't know about the pregnancy. I barely knew about the pregnancy and the doctor just confirmed that there was no longer a baby inside of me and potentially no baby ever! I had no reason to call Jamel and inform him about a thing. I really didn't even know where to find him. Everything really happened on a whim. My friend Estelle really wanted me to join in on the "Popped Cherry Squad," so she set me up with her caramel-apple skinned, oh-so-fine cousin Jamel, who was clearly twenty-five in the face, but only nineteen in earned years, to initiate me into womanhood. Initially, I was unsure about the entire situation. I prided myself on staying a virgin for so long, although my father was the sole reason. I still felt an air of self-respect and dignity. Most of the girls in my senior class lost their virginity in middle school around 7th and 8th grade. By high school, they were experimenting with sex toys and exchanging sex partners. I was curious, but no fool. In addition to their treasure chest of experience, they all knew the direct route to the women's clinic because they had been diagnosed with their fair share of sexually transmitted diseases. Out of all of them, I'm certain that somebody from my school was a living example of how to treat it.

Samson dropped me off at Estelle's mama's house in North

Oakland off 40th street and we walked, what seemed like a two-mile distance around the block to her aunt's one-story single-family house on the northwest border, where Jamel was patiently waiting our appointment. On the way over, Estelle filled me up with all of her Essence, Ebony and Jet Magazine's advice on the dos and don'ts of good lovemaking. She shared infinite wisdom on typical sex positions for amateurs, and how to actively respond to his touch. I imagined she thought she was "putting me up on game," but all she managed to do was make me even more nervous. I attempted to turn back several times, not taking my divine way of escape, knowing that what I was about to do was not truly in my heart. I didn't love this boy. *Wasn't sex supposed to be accompanied by love?* At least, that is the way my parents told it to me. My mother's advice was always to wait until you are old enough to deal with the consequences of intercourse, mentally, physically, spiritually, and medically. She found it hysterical to throw in the medical part with a wink and a "you know what I am talking about." Love will make you ready is what she always ended with. "What me and your father have is true love. Someday you will know what I mean." Honestly, if love is what they had, I wasn't interested.

I knew I wasn't in love, walking to his house. There had to be a better way in this scenario. No pregame date with dinner and flowers, just straight to the nightcap. I was certainly not a whore; so why did I feel so cheap? Yet, he was extremely handsome and attractive. He actually agreed to be intimate with me. This man had all the little *hoochies* on the block on his jock ready to make a 100-meter dash to his spot on command. I was doing him no favor. Every time he came around, my body tingled and my panties got moist. I was drunk off the juice too! It baffled me why this was occurring, but I enjoyed it and let it happen each and every time. I often plotted ways to get next to him, I even went as far to pretend I was cold—occasionally—so he would lend me his jacket, when he was no longer around, my clothes would carry a remnant of his Curve cologne goodness. He knew I was checking for him and played into it each time. His hand constantly brushed against my body "accidentally," as he claimed, but we both knew the innocent game we were playing. In spite of all of this, I wasn't prepared to take anything to the next level. But I was here now; there would be no turning back.

We did the final make-up, breath, and booty check; the one where you make sure it is still nice and on point as it was when you left the house and I was on the doorstep ringing the bell to get in and "get it in." He had bumping on the stereo, R. Kelly's *12 Play*; he was too ready. He wasted little time answering the doorbell on the first ring. His 5'11 185lb frame stood before me with his glistening, lightly chiseled chest welcoming to reach out and have a rub or two. I cautioned myself and subjected myself to taking mental pictures that would enhance my dreaming experience that night. It was clear he had just hopped out of the shower and threw on a towel to cover his slowly growing bulge, as to not make it too awkward before the real festivities started.

"Debra...Debra...Ms. Tucker. Are you OK? Do you need a moment?" Dr. White was out of her patience and ready to move on to her next patient.

"Just try my mother again. Call her cell this time."

"Without the consent of your legal guardian, we are incapable of discharging you." Dr. White reminded and buzzed for Ana attempting to get my mother on the line again.

# Chapter 7

The light knocking on the door startled Raquel from her midday meditation. This came when she had downtime between clients and she could focus her energy on staying positive and centered. With her wide array of clientele, from the high and mighty, pretentious clients to the modest tell-it-all customers, all left her with too much information and not enough evidence. It often weighed on her conscience, absorbing loads of gossip, recognizing that the subjects of the majority of the chatter had once been seated in her very chair. She was a spiritual woman. She knew there was a higher power and orchestrator of all good things in her life, but she was just not the churchgoing type. Meditation was her daily religion. In spite of her desire to remain undisturbed, she authorized her guest to come on in, hoping it wasn't anything too drastic to pull her from her tranquil state. With the recent line of events in her life concerning her son, she was rightfully on edge.

"Hey Beautiful. Can I come in?" Raquel, surprised at her visitor, reluctantly nodded and motioned her arm in the direction of the available seat. Instead, he walked around to where she was resting and hovered over her with preoccupation. "Baby, I need you to do me this favor one time. You know I wouldn't ask if it wasn't important."

Raquel was a bit flustered by his desperation and close proximity; however, she managed to keep her cool, maintaining a calm composure. "First of all, don't come in here sweet-talking me, you know we don't get down like that." Raquel moved her shoulder to avoid him from kissing her on her cheek. She knew it was coming because he always liked to sneak in quick kisses when she least expected it. She got up swiftly, moving around her salon office to keep a tolerable distance. His audacious, smooth-smelling cologne filled the room, sending charges through her worn out body, rejuvenating her in ways she was ill prepared to handle. It was necessary to stay at a fair distance to keep any unwanted sparks from flying between the two of them. "Now you know I don't get down with you like that and I would hate for your wife to walk in and think something is up. We have an agreement and I am sticking to my end of it." Raquel twisted up her face and body, displaying her disgust for him barging into her sanctuary to stir up buried feelings.

"I understand all of that, but Charlene is good with you. We put all the drama to rest years ago, but now I have some bigger fish to fry. I messed up and I need you."

"What happened?" She placed her hand on her hip. She made it a point to sound uninviting, to allow her vexation with his wavering pattern of behavior shine through.

Edmond finally pulled out one of her leather chairs and made himself comfortable. He sat back and propped his feet up, crossed his arms to get straight to the business at hand. "We had a huge blow-up the other day and I want to do something really special for her, plus our anniversary is right around the corner. I was thinking… a little pampering with hair, nails and make-up, then dinner at *The Crown Room* in the city, You know the sleek and sexy rooftop bar?" he stated making a rhetorical remark with the intention of stirring up some jealousy.

Raquel was in no way impressed by his attempt to make her jealous. It was almost embarrassing to her that he always managed to crawl back into her oasis when things went awry with his wife. "Ed...babe, spare me the details. You want me to believe that you came all the way down here to ask a favor? I understand you want the best for her, so you came to the best in town, but you best believe I am charging you full-price and I expect a hefty tip. And if she even attempts to get buck with me, I will burn off her edges!" Raquel twisted her neck with every word, making sure he fully understood the conditions of their new covenant. If, in fact, he did come this way to utilize her services; she thought it best to be worth the blood, sweat, and tears.

"Baby, it's all good. That won't be necessary. She will be on her better behavior. I promise. In fact, here is my down payment." He pulled out a bundle of crisp one hundred-dollar bills, counted out five Benjamins, and placed them on her oversize desk. "That should be enough for an appointment and for you a spa day, because you look stressed." He knew he didn't want to overstay his welcome and lead any of the gossiping women in the salon to jump to any more conclusions than they had already. He rested on his feet to begin his exit. Raquel summoned Tanya through the intercom to set up the appointment for Charlene Tucker.

"I must admit, Mr. Tucker; you are still looking and smelling good." Raquel followed her words with an examination of his muscular frame from head to toe. He kept in great shape. He may not have been able to get down like the young men, but he definitely held his own. "If Charlene decides that she doesn't want to deal with your mess anymore, you know where to find me. I will put a few of my beaus on the bench for you. It would be just like old times," she said with a smirk and wink, turning slightly for him to get a glimpse of her well-kept, voluptuous physique.

Her flirtation was becoming very reminiscent of the time when they had first met junior year of high school.

Raquel and Edmond were both exceptional athletes, part of the Fremont High School Varsity Track team. One day after practice, Edmond mustered up enough courage to finally ask her out. It was popular at the time to go steady with the girls who were the prettiest and, frankly, the most developed. Only the boys with the most "cool" had the ability to win the attention of these often-snooty girls. His boys made a bet with him that he didn't have a chance with Raquel and ultimately she would turn him down. Her trendy sense of style and grown woman curves made her a high commodity amongst the young boys in the school and around the neighborhood. She embodied the true definition of LL Cool J's *Around the Way Girl*. When Edmond was able to swoop her up, all the fellas knew that he was the man. She dropped her nineteen-year-old boyfriend at the time to be with him. Neither of them knew that just a year later, Charles would come and turn their world upside down.

The original plan was to ask her out, win the bet and drop her for the next lady that caught his eye, yet it did not quite pan out that way; for some reason she stuck around, he didn't know love at the time, but it was the closest thing to it. Dating in high school was rough. Edmond spent a lot of time playing ball with his boys at the local parks, in his mind trying to stay distant from Raquel to avoid becoming too attached. He loved her and enjoyed her company, but now that they were seniors, he wanted to make sure he could keep his options open. His boys were in the habit of keeping the company of several women, and he didn't want to be the only one tied down.

However, Raquel was no dunce. She could sense the fact that Edmond was distancing himself from her. During this time, her ex-boyfriend was attempting to make a comeback in her life. She was lonely, and fighting it became less and less of an obligation. One day, her willpower to avoid her attraction left her remorseful, lost in a predicament of commitment to an unborn child. She was caught between one man that really only wanted her body, not her heart, and another who was gradually slipping away. Edmond was the type of man to never run from any challenge. In fact, he often welcomed it. Finding out that his high school sweetheart was pregnant nearly broke him, yet he gave his word to be there for her no matter what the outcome. He worked extra jobs just to help her make ends meet. He even sacrificed his dedicated time with his boys to help with babysitting. He was truly invested for the long haul.

Things turned sour quick. Time together became fewer and far between. Raquel had a difficult time raising her son and attending cosmetology school. Her mother refused to assist in the child-rearing process, claiming her responsibility was to Raquel not her child. She was adamant about the fact that her job was complete and she had no desire to commence yet again. Edmond made it his duty to ensure that cash would never be a burden for her and picked up their son when he could. He was raised to be a man and work to support his family, no matter what the cost. He paid the majority of her schooling and expenses. Her ambition for success encouraged him to get back into school, so he enrolled in Merritt Community College.

The vibration from her cell phone suspended her reliving of the past. She glanced over at the phone and realized their time had been well spent.

"And thank you for coming down to the courthouse. I knew that his no-good daddy wouldn't do anything, so I didn't bother calling. Charles still doesn't know who he is. You always kept your word to stay in his life. You are the only father he knows. For that, I'll do anything for you." Raquel felt herself getting sentimental. "Hurry up and get out of here before you start something up." This time, she allowed him gently kiss her forehead as they parted ways. He grabbed her in his arms and held her in a tight embrace for a moment, long enough to savor her floral fragrance, reminiscing about the times they would hold each other. After a moment, he let her go and walked out of her office.

Tanya didn't waste a moment dashing into the office after the coast was clear. "Guurrrl, who was that?" she asked, waiting in suspense, wanting to digest the new dirt.

"Child please! That was old news walking out the door. That was the heartbreaker I told you about from my younger days." She rolled her eyes a bit, playing back in her head what she had just spoken.

"Well, it sure seemed to me that news is current!" Tanya instigated while she made herself comfortable in the very chair he got up from, still warm from the energy he emitted from his core.

"Ed and I had some good times back in the day. I could always count on him; at least until he started making a life for himself.

He met that woman and things changed. I refused to share him, so I ended it with him." Raquel shook her head and stared off into the wall for a moment again, feeling herself becoming emotional. "But never mind all that anyway. His wife will be in for her appointment, so just don't mention anything that happened today. We have an agreement, and I want to make sure I keep up my end."

"If you say so, boss! All I know is what I witnessed… that man is clearly not over you. Wife or not, you had him first! If I were you…"

Raquel quickly interjected. "Honey, you are not me. You are still a young thang, wet behind the ears. You don't know a thing about keeping a man. Little girl, you probably haven't even had a real orgasm yet. Let me be the teacher in *this* shop and you take notes. How you get them is how you have to keep them. He comes when I need him, and that is all you need to know. Your break is officially over! Please get my next client prepped." Tanya sensed she had overstepped her boundaries and took her cue to leave before she stirred up any more mess.

Raquel's cell phone vibrated on the desk again. She knew that it must be important. Her heart began to beat a little faster. She swallowed hard before answering. She remained silent to allow them to speak first.

"Hello." The deep voice echoed in her ear. "Are you alone?"

"Yes. Tanya just walked out of my office."

"I miss you. When can I see you again?" The caller spoke with an unruffled nature, yet still an air of demand in his request. Raquel was conscious that her time was running out, and she needed to make good on her promise.

"I can see you tonight, but it will be late. I still have three heads left."

75

"Good. Meet me at the Marriott Hotel in downtown when you are finished. I will text you the room number. And wear something sexy." He moaned after his last word with a kiss through the phone and hung up.

Raquel flopped back in her executive chair, closed her eyes in meditation. She was going to need some truly divine intervention to see her through this situation.

It was a quarter after eight and Raquel was exhausted, yet she knew that this meet up was necessary. After her last client left the shop, she immediately wiped down the stations, swept the floor, folded the freshly washed towels and was out the door. Normally, the cleaning would be left for Tanya, but she allowed her to go home early because she was feeling under the weather. Raquel was not above cleaning duties. It was imperative for the salon to remain immaculate at all times. She had a standard to uphold. Quality hair had no place in a filthy shop, in addition to the fact that her creative innovation thrived on cleanliness.

Once the trash was emptied, she was all set for her evening. Not having enough time to go through her date preparation routine; complete with a warm bubble bath, wash, blow dry, flat iron plus styling of her hair and full application of make-up, she settled for a quick birdbath via her bathroom sink. She used her curling iron to bump the few curls that dropped due to the work of the day. She slipped on her little black dress, always ready for her late night excursions that sang classy yet sexy-sophisticated. The outfit was not complete without *Ralph Lauren's* Romance perfume strategically applied to the special parts of her body that always made her male suitors weak in the knees. Raquel took one last look in the full body mirror; she had to admit that she looked good. Being forty-eight never stopped her one bit. It gave her more confidence that she looked good for her age. Most men mistook her for her early thirties. She set the alarm system and was on her way.

On the ride over to the hotel, she couldn't help thinking about Charles. For some reason, he was pulling on her heartstrings. Most of the time, she awaited his call because it was always on time with some sort of request for deliverance. She dialed his number from her Bluetooth, that made driving and handling business calls more convenient when she was pressed for time. His phone rang a few times before his voicemail picked up.

"You know who this is and you know what to do. Holla at me at the beep." *Beep*!

"Hey Pook! It's Mama. You were on my mind, so I called. Well, I guess you are busy, probably with some heifer. Don't bother calling back. I'll be out. Come by and see me tomorrow. Love you, son."

The Marriott was just the way she left it the last time she had a late night rendezvous. She parked in the guest overnight parking to avoid having to valet in the front of the building. It was nobody's business why she was there or who she was there to see. She conducted her final face and breath check, inhaled all of her frustrations, irritations and disappointment and exhaled her guilt and regret. This night was predetermined, necessary. She whispered a quick prayer to herself.

*Lord, you know all about it. I'm not perfect, but I gotta do what I gotta do. Just watch over me. In Jesus' name, Amen.*

She grabbed her silver Michael Kors clutch to match her silver pumps. She checked to make sure her pepper spray was still tucked away in the crevice of the inner pocket to use in the event of an emergency.

Luckily, the lobby remained primarily inactive. The hotel was selected for its proximity to the downtown area, if the desire was to go out for a night on the town full of drinking and dancing. The best part is that it catered to those traveling for business. It was very unlikely to run into locals that would ask a million questions about why you are staying in a hotel within the city that you reside. It would make one think to themselves why they are so concerned, considering they are in the same predicament. Raquel made her way to the elevators. She pressed the button to go up to the seventh floor to room 731, just as she was instructed to do. She admired herself through the reflection of the elevator doors. *Damn, I look good!*

"Raquel? Girl, is that you?" She was discovered, but by who? What were the odds that of all the nights she would run into someone she knew, in this hotel and this late? "Raquel, I know that is you." The voice rang out.

Raquel slowly made an about face to greet the all too familiar voice. "Hey Lydia." she greeted with as much enthusiasm as she could muster up, which wasn't any.

"You look…" she looked her up and down, fishing for the words to complete her sentence.

"I look good! I know that is what you were trying to say." The sass from Raquel was beginning to emerge.

"I see you haven't changed any." Lydia added an extra perusal of her countenance and cut her eyes. "What brings you out so late? Still bed hopping like you used to do back in the day?"

"First of all, that is none of your business! I am a grown woman and make my own decisions. Be clear, I am not ashamed, which is more than you can say for yourself." Raquel felt herself getting upset, taking her back to a time in her life that she worked hard every day to move away from.

"I'm just kidding with you, Rocky. Calm down. We are grown women now and just like you said, all that is in the past. I don't even speak to Charlene anymore. You have probably heard more from her than I have. After I had Lance, or when I found out I was pregnant, I stopped coming around as much. I didn't want her to feel some type of way since she was having her own issues getting pregnant." The elevator chimed to let Raquel know it was ready. She decided to let it go on. This was a conversation she needed to have.

"Well, that makes two of us. I only speak to her when I have to or when Ed makes me. Considering our boys are so close, you would think that even *we* would have a better relationship." Raquel sighed. "Well, we all know you ain't never had no man stick around, so the jury is still out on your miracle baby." Raquel laughed at her own humor. "Now, since you are all up in my business; why are you here?"

"The only men my world revolves around are my son and my Jesus. I don't need nobody else!" She looked up at the sky and waved her hallelujah hands. "But, anyway... Bank of America is having a conference here at the hotel and I never go away, so I decided to use this as a mini-vacation, staying at the hotel overnight like an out-of-towner." Lydia was proud. It was clear that she was unable to travel and get away much. Since she was often consumed with Lance's life, she felt she might miss something; or worse, something happen and she wouldn't be right there to save him. "Let me not hold you up, though. By the looks of it, I don't want you to keep that man waiting." She smirked, trying to maintain her serious face. Raquel only rolled her eyes in response. "By the way, how is Charles? I overheard Lance talking to him the other day when he came by the house. Is everything all right? Although I may not care for you at times, I do love your son like he is my own."

"I bet you do." Raquel tried her best to be polite and courteous, but she did not care about Lydia and her sneaky ways. She tried to put on to the world that she was a new woman, saved, sanctified and filled with the Holy Ghost, but Raquel knew otherwise. However, it was true, their sons were like brothers and she had the same love for Lance. "Charles is good. He got himself into a little trouble, but nothing that can't be fixed." The chiming sound of the elevator reminded her of her task at hand, and with that, Raquel hurried into the open elevator just in time for her to make her exit. She didn't bother saying goodbye. Lydia was more than capable of knowing that their conversation was over.

The elevator seemed to take an eternity to reach the seventh floor. She glanced at her watch to see if the time was far later than she planned to arrive, and it was. Everything was already set in motion—no need to turn back. Three light taps on the door were all it took, and the door was opened. Rose petals painted the pathway of the modestly sized suite leading to the king-sized bed.

"I almost thought you were going to stand me up." The deep, gentle voice sent immediate chills through her body. She was reminded why all of this was necessary and worth the hassle. He poured her a glass of red wine to calm her nerves. It was apparent that she was a bit uneasy about the whole ordeal that transpired downstairs. He gently kissed her forehead and moved down to her neck and shoulder.

"Your Honor? Hold up one moment." Things were moving so fast it slipped out. Things were going faster than she expected. His soft touch was a bit overwhelming, but appreciated.

"In here, you can call me Fred. I'm not judging the case in here. It is just us, so no formalities. I'm not 'Your Honor' or Judge Price. None of that." He removed the glass from her grip and placed it on the nightstand next to the bed. He used his hands to alleviate the tension in her shoulders. In between massage patterns, he placed light kisses on her neck and ear until he could feel her body begin to synchronize to his body rhythm. "I know this may be a little difficult for you, but trust me. When your son is cleared of all the charges, it will be all worth it. Plus, I like you. This doesn't have to be a onetime agreement." Raquel zoned out. His words became a faint sound in her subconscious, catapulting her into a quiet place of relaxation and ecstasy. She laid back, closed her eyes, and let him take full advantage of her.

"Housekeeping!" Raquel lifted her head above the covers to check the time. All of her released tension exhausted her body, and she didn't realize that she slept fully through the night. It had been her practice to get out of dodge before the rising of the sun if she could. To her surprise, her late night lover had beat her to the punch. Judge Price had cleared the hotel room, leaving a note behind on the nightstand accompanied with small breakfast and a cup of black coffee.

*It was nice. Thank you! You took care of me, so I will take care of*
*you!*
*Fred*

Although she felt a little cheap on the inside, it was well worth it. Judge Frederick Price was the ideal man to commit this type of crime with. He was tall, dark and handsome and knew exactly how to use what God gave him, even if he did not give it to him to be used in that way. Raquel smiled to herself, knowing that she could check off one less problem, considering her son seemed to always fall at the top of the problem list. It was imperative for her to clean off her sins before leaving the hotel. She turned on the water to the hottest temperature she could withstand and hopped in. She whispered another word of prayer as the water ran down her body.

The faint sounds of DMX's voice sounded through the bathroom walls. Charles had finally decided to call her back. However, with all the activity from last night and the fact she was a little tipsy, he could have called her back then without her knowledge. She grabbed her towel after she was thoroughly clean and checked her voicemail.

"Mama… Elijah is dead! I am trying my best not to bust a cap in someone's ass. I can't promise what I might do. I think I know who did this. It's all my fault. Don't call me back… I love you!"

Charles meant business. When he spoke in that manner, there was no convincing him otherwise. *How is it that I get him out of one situation and he falls into another? I can't do this anymore!* She immediately called back to be directed to his voicemail. Again and again, she attempted to get him to pick up. *Voicemail. Voicemail. Voicemail.* She even aimed to get Lance on the line, but all she received was a disconnected message. It had been a time since she tried to reach him, so she figured he probably had his number changed. She had no other choice than to make that unwanted call.

Her hand trembled as each ring reverberated in her ear. She dreaded the day when she would have to call for his help. After all, he made no attempt to be there for her or his son after Edmond became a staple in her life. This time, it was not for her to call on Edmond and jeopardize his whole family because of Charles. Now was time for his father to step up and shut all this mess down once and for all.

When it appeared as though the voicemail trend was going to be the theme of the day, he answered.

"Hello... Calvin... it's me Rocky. I'm calling about your son."

# Chapter 8

They pulled up to the quaint 24-hour diner nestled on the corner of West Grand and Broadway. It was just after midnight and both Jamie Lynn and Lance were exhausted and hungry. The events of the evening created a void in their stomachs that was yearning for fulfillment. She turned down the evening's soundtrack of slow jams, pulled her vehicle up into the open slot that was awaiting her arrival and placed the car in park. She held back a brief period before engaging Lance. For her, this fared the perfect opportunity to talk without any interruptions—no engine rumbling and no crazy women.

"What was all of that about back there? That girl was crazy if she thought I was going to get out of the car and fight her. I stopped fighting chicks in high school." She spat out her question, following each word with a twist and turn of her neck, ending with her arms folded and her lips pooched out to the side.

"Okay. I see you, Miss Sassy!" Lance chuckled a bit at her attempt to be forceful. To him, she seemed so delicate. Her sophisticated appearance and aura made it difficult for him to believe that she even got into verbal spars with anyone. Yet he was impressed by the way she maneuvered the car and had his back when she barely knew him at all. "I like your style."

He reached over and put his hand on the back of her neck, massaging and rubbing her smooth soft skin. He stared at her with his soothing brown eyes, captivating her attention, attempting to look deep into her eyes to read her energy. She was such a beautiful woman, Lance thought to himself. Any man would be lucky to have her in their arms. He thought about how he reacted to his mom earlier and how she had done him a solid by requesting her to meet him down at the bar. The moment was magical. He could feel that she was into him, but he knew it was best to take things slow. He was always so hasty with getting intimate with the women he entertained. In fact, the only reason he entertained the women in his life thus far was for the sex. It was his release, his getaway from the trials and tribulations of life. Yet and still an obvious weakness.

Jamie couldn't help herself; her blushing and slight jitters gave it away. She was digging him. For her, it was more of a treat because he was desired by other women and in her eyes; he was choosing her, even if only for the moment. She was a reserved type of girl, but in the hands of the right man, she would transform to be his every fantasy.

Her value and worth were important to her, so she was hesitant to jump in the bed with men she was not in a committed relationship with. She had seen so much in her lifetime that it made her cautious when dealing with men. Her father never married her mother, and he brought around woman after woman with no desire or intention to live in holy matrimony. He revealed to her the mind of the man and the manipulation that they were capable of. *Men only want one thing and if they tell you otherwise, it's a lie.* His words constantly rang in her mind. Although she was abreast of the game, it was still difficult to deny her emotions, her desires. His touch made her comfortable. For some reason, he calmed her soul. However, she remained committed to her game plan.

"What's on your mind?" Lance broke the silence as if he could read her thoughts still caressing her hair and neck.

"I'm just hungry. Let's get in this diner so we can eat." The moment was too good to ruin it with talking about his previous relationships and poor taste in women. She tabled the conversation for another day and didn't press the fact that he avoided her questions all together. Jamie Lynn motioned to open her door. When he stopped her, promptly hopped out to be the newly revived, chivalrous man and open the door for her.

His personal cell vibrated in his pocket. He closed her door and took a quick glance at the caller ID. Seeing it was Charles—he sent him to voicemail. He couldn't afford any more interruptions this evening. His time profited him to be occupied with his new lady. He gracefully slipped his hand into her hand, locking fingers as he escorted her into the restaurant as a message to any eligible bachelors in the vicinity that this woman was off the market; even if he had not purchased yet. He didn't want to give her any more ammunition to blow off this evening before it had truly gotten started. He vowed to give her his undivided attention for as long as possible.

Once more, his phone vibrated, this time his alternate phone. The Metro PCS phone he gave out to the hoodrats he met. Charles again. Charles had a rule about being on the phone with another man. If it didn't involve moneymaking or hustling, it was an emergency. Lance took the risk, sending him to voicemail again, hoping he would just leave a message for him to check later once they got settled inside, or at least after he secured that the evening would not bring about a nightcap. The phone chirped, alerting him that Charles did as he preferred.

They found a nice, quiet booth in the diner and made themselves comfortable. The diner wasn't too fancy, more urban chic. The reviews described the place as a late night hot spot for good food at a decent price. Lance was a stickler for good food. If his mama wasn't the chef, it had to be Grade A. The price was not a concern of his, as he made it a point to treat his ladies to the finest of dining.

There were a few couples scattered about the place, engrossed in conversation over half-eaten meals, waiting for the chance to devour the remnants once they reached their key point. In order to expedite the ordering process, Jamie Lynn excused herself to the ladies' room to freshen up. She instructed Lance to order her something he thought she would like with an ice water and lemon. Now alone, Lance counted this the perfect opportunity to check his message from Charles.

"Lance, they shot him! He's dead. Elijah is dead! Bruh, where you at? I can't believe this is happening… Meet me at the crib when you get this message… Gone." *Click.* You could hear the outrage and desperation in his voice. He was fighting back tears, gagging on his words. The message didn't provide answers. It was broken in meaning. There were too many unanswered questions.

Lance froze. He replayed the message repeatedly to ensure he was not having a nightmare. He couldn't believe what he was hearing. Each time, the message produced the same outcome. A tingling shot up his back, in his hands and feet. He didn't know how to receive the news he was hearing.

Straightaway, he got up and started pacing back and forth.

He was shaking his head, switching his hands from his head to his side with balled up fists swinging through the air. He grabbed glasses, silverware, napkin holders, salt and pepper shakers; one by one from his table as well as nearby tables and flung them across the room. His anger was out of his control. He no longer had a grip on his emotions. He located the wall and hammered his right fist through the drywall, leaving a melon-sized hole.

The patrons in the restaurant just stood back and observed. They kept their distance, sensing that he was capable of destroying anything that came his way. You could hear their whispers of disgust for a black man misbehaving in this manner in a public restaurant, without knowledge of the motive fueling his outrage. The owner of the diner wasted no time getting the local police on the line to assist in defusing the situation. With each toss of the table decorations, he shouted expletives, still punching the air space that stood in his path. His confusion overtook him. He was just with his friend moments before. He was his ride to The Shadow Bar to release his stress; and just like that, he was gone. No goodbye or farewell. He was stripped of his opportunity of life. And just with a snap of a finger, he stopped. He dropped the contents that lay waiting in his palm for release. He had nothing left in him.

As soon as Jamie Lynn returned from the restroom, she sensed his change in demeanor. The fact that he had his back turned, standing with no movement, startled her. She surveyed her surroundings. She cautiously approached him, but she stayed far enough to manage a safe distance away from his awkward behavior.

"Lance, are you okay? What's wrong?" Lance didn't speak any words to her. He stayed put with a blank stare. She ran to his aid, hoping he would answer and remove the distress she was experiencing on his behalf. He stood silent, his fists stilled, balled. She had no other choice but to embrace him. His body instantly folded in her arms. His body weight overwhelmed her as she gently buckled to the floor with him still in her arms. He cried for the first time in years.

In most situations, he was able to overcome without a flinch. This time was different. Elijah was one of his closest friends, his mentor, confidant, and brother. He was the last person he imagined something like this happening to. He didn't have enemies. He worked too hard in the community to build relationships with the people in his circle. He was their protector, though. He made sure that the enemies that wanted their blood kept their distance. Jamie kept him in her embrace, whispering *everything will be OK* as she caressed the crown of his head and wiped away his tears.

The police sirens were loud outside the diner. Three officers barreled in the establishment, headed in his direction under the advisement of the owner. One officer had his gun drawn slowly moving in his direction, while the other officers trailed behind, ready for the command of the leading officer.

"Excuse me, sir? Is there a problem we can help you with? We received a call that there was a disturbance." The leading officer requested.

Lance didn't budge. He remained in her arms, hoping that they would get the hint that he had calmed down and depart to handle more important business.

"Excuse me, sir, but I am going to have to ask you to leave. It looks like you have done some damage here and by the request of the owner; we need you to vacate the premises." The officer was patient. He lowered his gun in recognition that he was not an imposing threat and provided wait time for Lance to comprehend his request and comply.

"Where were you when my boy got shot, huh? Did you even show up at the scene? But yet you are here giving me a hard time and I haven't done anything to anyone," Lance replied as his anger welled up inside of him.

Jamie Lynn interjected. "I'm so sorry, officer; but he is grieving. I will pay for whatever is damaged. Can you just give us a moment and we will be out of here? All of these officers are unnecessary. He is harmless." She gave a look to the owner, hoping he would honor her request and call off the dogs. The owner saw the sincerity in her and obliged.

"Thank you, officers, for coming down and responding, but I think everything is okay now."

It was obvious the leading officer wanted to make some form of an arrest. It was written all over his face, but since the owner decided that he didn't want to press charges, they had no jurisdiction and evacuated the premises.

Lance still lay helpless in Jamie's arms as she remained clueless about the event that led to his breakdown.

"You gotta talk to me, babe," she whispered to him. "I want to be able to be here for you." Lance slowly lifted his head to meet her eyes head on.

"My boy Elijah just got shot. They shot him! He's dead. He didn't do anything, and they killed him." Jamie Lynn was even more confused. So many thoughts ran through her brain. *What was he really into? Was someone after them? Did she get herself involved in some mess?*

"Who shot him?" she requested, trying to get some answers that would provide clarity to the situation.

"I'm not sure, but I think I know who it was."

"Who? Lance, you have to talk to me." Jamie Lynn was a bit frightened; it was more than she really bargained for. Multiple women in his life she could deal with, but death and violence were all too reminiscent of her childhood that she fought so hard to distance herself from.

"I don't want to get you caught up in this!"

"I'm already in it. I'm here!" she pleaded.

"I don't want to talk about it. Just get me out of here. I need to get to my boys. I wasn't there when it went down. I wasn't able to protect him like he has always protected me. Nah...I'm too busy tryin' to smash." He was beginning to work himself up again. The owner of the diner kept a close watch on him, periodically glancing at the clock on the wall and the phone as if he was sending a telepathic message to Jamie that her grace period was about to run out. She was well aware and kick started "Operation Get Ghost."

"I know that you are upset, but there is nothing that you could have done. Let's just get out of here while we still have a chance. I'll take you wherever you need to go, but you gotta tell me who did this. I may be able to help." She held his face in the palm of her hand, reassuring him that she was on his team.

Lance just stared blankly back at her. What could she possibly do to help? He had already put her through so much and they had just met hours ago. The simplicity of his evening became tarnished with one phone call. He couldn't help but place the blame on himself. Had he not called Elijah to pick him up, he would still be alive. Yet, again, the vibration of his phone suspended his thoughts. Wrapped up in his thoughts, he didn't recognize the number and just picked up the call. At this point, it could have been anyone. He couldn't risk missing an opportunity to be present this time around.

"Hello. What's up? Who is this?"

"Lance, it's me Darnise. I heard what happened. The block is real hot right now. Baby, come home. You know I got you. I don't care about the girl you are with. I know us. I rocked with Elijah too. I'll be up waiting."

"Bet. Gone." He hung up the phone. He proceeded to give the directions to Jamie about where to drop him off. The ride was silent, no music, no conversation. There was too much tension in the air. Lance couldn't trust Jamie. He had just met her, but Darnise was familiar; he knew what to expect. She understood her role and for him, that was his best and only option.

# Chapter 9

T he hospital was still fairly busy, although the evening was winding down. Ana was completing her necessary paperwork to end her shift when Charlene came strolling in. Her hair was disheveled, and she was wearing the same outfit from the day prior. She was too tired to care what anyone had to say about it. She was still disappointed that she had to take another turnaround trip down to Riverside. Nevertheless, she was concerned about her baby girl.

She received the unwelcome call from Dr. White while at Big Mama's house, where she only planned to stay for a few days while she cleared things up with Edmond. Spending a day away from her loved one was grueling to her soul. However, she had to tough it out, if he was to have any clue of the impact his actions had on her. She was making her stand through her pain, hurt, and frustration. Through it all, she found her voice, and she felt empowered.

Big Mama was displeased with her actions and wanted her quickly to go back and apologize to her husband for stepping out of line. Big Mama believed that when a man is chastising his son, a mother is to stay out of it and in her place. She basically held on to the sentiment that women were to be submissive at all times, especially if the man was financially supporting the household. Her daughter didn't have a stream of income that would support her if anything were to happen. Housing her adult daughter due to her own admission was not what Mrs. Anita White-Whitfield was going to tolerate.

The call from the doctor did not alleviate her situation. It caught her by surprise. She thought, just as her husband believed, that their little girl was still pure, not broken like them. They attempted every means to keep their children away from suffering; and even so, life had its way of creeping in without warning and causing havoc. She informed the doctor that she would be on the next flight out to see about her daughter. She knew it was long overdue for her to share some things with Debra. As her mother passed along jewels of wisdom to her in her time of transition from adolescence to adulthood, it was time for her to do the same.

Charlene hesitated before walking into the room. She took in a deep breath and released it slowly, not knowing how Debra would receive her. The flight measured long enough for her to devise the perfect entrance, or so she thought. She previously missed her call as she fought to preserve the life of her first child. At the moment when she was needed most, she was bickering, at odds with her husband, creating a deeper wedge in their already toxic relationship. She was absent, not there in the way that she needed her to be. She even wrestled with the thought that maybe everything that had transpired with her daughter was her own fault. If she had only been there for her a little bit more, to speak with her about boys, the birds, and the bees. Instead, she left her alone, abandoned to make sense of the world through the lens of her peers and her personal encounters. She grabbed a bouquet of white lilies on her way in from the hospital gift shop as a peace offering, with the intention of striking a chord that would lead to harmony.

She tapped lightly on the door, not to startle her, but to notify her daughter. She had arrived, coming to her rescue. Without a response, she decided to let herself in. She placed the flowers on the small table that lay adjacent to her daughter's bed. Debra was asleep. Charlene could not wait a moment longer to get all of this hurt, pain, and animosity shared between the two of them out into the open and put it all to rest. She rolled over a chair to sit and wake her. Debra was normally a light sleeper, so it didn't take much for Charlene to get her up.

"Debra? Baby? I'm here. Mama's here for you." She stated with a bit of hesitation, nudging her lightly on her side.

"Mama? Is it really you? You came for me." I have to admit, I was shocked. I knew she would come, but I had my doubts, and she was alone. My mother didn't travel alone. Then I remembered the phone conversation the previous night with Samson. "Is everything alright with you and daddy?" I could see the hurt in her expression as soon as I finished the question; in a way, I almost regretted asking.

"That is what I would like to talk to you about. I spoke with the doctor and she informed me about everything. The 9-1-1 call, the pregnancy and the miscarriage." She waited a moment before continuing to keep herself from crying too soon. "I should have been there for you. I'm sorry. I hope that you can find it in your heart to forgive me." Tears began to well up in her eyes. She couldn't help herself. She gently wiped the corners of her eye with the back of her index finger knuckle to keep her makeup from running, although it was too late.

"Mama, it's okay. You are here now and that is all that matters." I hated to see her cry, or anyone else, for that matter. It always gave me this weird feeling, as if I was going to cry too, even if I was unable to relate or empathize with the pain. The time I spent lying in the hospital bed allowed for me to think several things over about life and family. Life is entirely too short to spend at odds with my own mother. I know she did the best she could with her ability.

"No, Debra. It is time that we discussed this. You are old enough now and, based on your current situation, you are mature enough to handle what I am going to share with you."

I wasn't sure where this conversation was heading. The feeling I experienced when the doctor was explaining her report was creeping up on me again, but I knew in my heart it was time. I decided to let her have the floor with no interruptions, so I could hear her out and understand how we got this far and where things went astray. I grabbed her hand, nodded, and she began.

"When I met your father, I was only eighteen years old. He was a very handsome, determined and sought-after young man. He was successful, and he took care of his business. It is what attracted me to him, along with the other women in school who had eyes and common sense. I knew he was in a relationship at the time, but for some reason, it didn't matter to me. The way he looked at me made me feel as if I was the only woman in his world. I wasn't, but that didn't matter. He gave me his time, his energy, his dreams. He allowed me into his soul. At the beginning of our relationship, I was tolerant of many things. I knew he was a young man who was not ready to settle down, and I wasn't sure if that was what I wanted either, so we were content with what we had. The other woman that your father was dating at the time had a 3-year-old son. We were not officially dating, but we had created a deep bond and friendship. He confided in me. Edmond was excited about being a father until the day he found out that it wasn't his. He was devastated. I was there each and every day to pick up the broken pieces of his heart. It devastated him that he was not the father and, in many ways, he was unsure how to cope with it. He turned to alcohol when things really got tough."

"Mama, I don't think I want to know this. What does this have to do with my situation?" I could feel my body slightly trembling as she got deeper into the story. I made it a point to avoid knowing their business. What I knew already was enough for me. Nonetheless, she continued.

"Your father felt betrayed by this woman and it almost ruined him. But I was there! I was there!" Her voiced raised slightly to add emphasis. She was no longer looking at me; her eyes were affixed on the drapes, but her mind was elsewhere. "Your father did a lot of dirt in his day to provide a stable home for both families. At times, he was lost and confused. He went back and forth between me and her for a while and I allowed it. I knew that he loved me and we had true love. I despised that woman. She took a piece of my man that I fought years to get back, to restore. He longed for that child. I let him go and stay with her at times, if only for a moment; so he could have that piece of his life. However, I knew that he would ultimately be mine and that he would be my husband. I knew what I had to do; I had to get pregnant. I had to conceive a child of my own and everything would get better. I did things I never even shared with your father. So many times, I was unable to carry a baby to term. I had several miscarriages to the point it was taking a toll on him even more. So I researched fertility options. My best friend at the time agreed to be my surrogate, but that failed because she was taking anti-depressants and the embryo died within the first week. I would like to say after much prayer, finally, I got pregnant, but I didn't pray about it. I went about everything the wrong way. Samson was my miracle baby though; I was twenty-five when he was born. The doctors thought that he was dead when I delivered him. Debra, it was the happiest moment of my life because I knew that I would be granted the life I dreamed of; the man who was my soul mate would finally take me as his wife. You see, he was hesitant to marry me without the possibility of a family. The day Samson came into the world, our lives changed, for the better… and then the worse." A stream of tears rolled down my mother's face; her hands were trembling.

Until this moment, I had never witnessed her so transparent, so real. I caressed her hand to let her know that I was there for her and it was safe to continue. It was becoming evident to me why all of this was necessary, why she treated Samson the way she did. He was her ticket; he equated a world of bliss for her.

She dabbed her eyes to catch the newly forming tears. "I didn't plan to get pregnant with you a year and a half later. Money was tight for a while. Our relationship was up and down, a roller coaster, and yet again, your father was in and out of the house. So I resented you for it. I thought if I could just focus on Samson and get him right that things would get better and I would have the wedding and marriage I always dreamed of." She shifted and faced me, looking directly into my eyes; "I want you to know that I love you and I never meant to hurt you in any way. You can come to me. We can work this out." There was nothing but silence; we felt one another's energy and love, and for the first time, we cried together, exposing our suffering. I didn't want the moment to end. I had been yearning for my mother's love and affection for so long I didn't know how to ask for it, so I acted out. I was not a bad or disrespectful child in any way, but I feel that all of this was a cry out for help.

We held each other and lay suspended in the moment. It all came to a sudden halt when the sound of my father's custom ringtone entered our atmosphere, our newly created alliance. My mother held me tighter, as though she was not concerned with the caller on the other end, but I couldn't stand for their feud to continue. Her transparency needed to be shared with my father. There was so much that I learned in our moment about the rise and fall of relationships, the evolution of love.

My father was persistent after each unanswered call; he made another attempt to get through. I watched my mother go through a range of emotions and contemplation. She would stare at the screen and shake her head, taking in a breath while holding back her tears. Over and over, the ringing sounded and engorged our room, our space. I knew she needed time, but time is what nearly severed our relationship our chance at happiness and trust. Again and again and again, the sound rang out from her android phone. Finally, after much struggle, she surrendered.

"Hello." She tried to keep her voice low to keep their conversation private. I couldn't hear my father, but I read everything through my mother, her words, and her emotions.

For her to show up, to put me, as the priority in her life is all I ever needed. Her existence in my life is all I cried out for, but it was my time to be there for her, to be her anchor. I held her up as she emptied out her contents to my father—no yelling, no cursing, no screaming, just conversation and apologies.

"I love you, Edmond. I will be home soon, right in time for our anniversary. We have a lot of making up to do." She blushed for the first time in years, at least by my own account.

I had a good feeling that things were destined to get better.

They had to. However, I knew it would begin with me getting out of the hospital.

Dr. White made it clear that everything was OK, and I was in good condition to go home. She stressed to me that there are some cases where it becomes difficult for women to have babies, but with the advancement of science, technology, and new alternatives that one-day, I may have the chance to have a baby. Both the doctor and I knew that it was much too soon for me to worry about it, anyway.

"Mama, just hurry up and sign those papers so we can go home."

# Chapter 10

His hands trembled as he released his grip from the revolver. His heart was beating out of his chest, proving to be the most terrifying and exhilarating encounter in his life. The still of the night painted the perfect scene for the homicide. His eyes finally opened to the reality of being a killer. He felt he was a coward to keep his eyes closed as the bullets blasted from the pistol. He took his assignment and executed it to the best of his novice ability. The perspiration from his chest and stomach soaked through his t-shirt.

Point. Aim. Shoot. He followed the simple instructions that resulted in the big payoff of ten thousand dollars—cash. Quite frankly, he didn't have a choice. His rights were given up the moment he stepped into the vehicle. He knew it would come at a cost. Deep down inside, he craved the sensation of taking a life. Endless nights of playing *Grand Theft Auto* failed to give this moment its true justice. Beads of sweat gathered on the top of his forehead, reminiscent of the blood that trickled from the lifeless body outside The Shadow Bar.

"Now you understand why you can't say a word about our dealings? This ain't no walk in the park, Young Blood," his voice strong and commanding, ensuring that his new young protégé was coherent. Calvin kept his eyes glued on Samson to monitor his behavior. The first killing was always the most difficult to experience. He needed to ensure that Samson could handle what he had done and wouldn't go running in the streets making any confessions. "He was a bad man, so he had to go. And you did it." Calvin removed the gun from Samson's fingertips, wiping it clear of any evidence of his prints. He didn't waste any time at the scene attempting to verify if the target was taken out—it was done.

The last thing Samson needed was for Calvin Rogers to think that the job duties were too difficult for him to carry out. He swallowed hard and offered him a nod to show his comprehension. He placed the wad of cash paid out to him for his services in his backpack, the backpack he relied on for every occasion. One of the first purchases with his earnings would be a Metro PCS cell phone, he figured with the new job it would require for him to be accessible at all times. His parents refused to get him a cellphone; they felt he had yet to show he had any responsible gene in his body. However, working with Mr. Rogers would allow him to bypass many of their unfair, biased rules.

The driver stopped one block shy of the newly remodeled apartment building downtown where Samson was crashing during his stint away from home. He longed to be back in the comfort of his own home, bed, living space, but he knew that the tension between him and his father was too thick to break through this soon. His father had a black belt in holding grudges and making you feel the pain of his wrath. Despite desiring alternative living arrangements, he would settle for his freedom being crammed into the cubical sized space his "lady-friend," not considered a girlfriend, called home, thwarting his sexual advances, due to her new found morality following their indecent exposure.

The chill of the night air layered upon the car windows, awaiting the midnight visitors to canvass the neighborhood. He crawled out of the warmth of the car, knowing that this was only the beginning of many more assignments. He felt proud, though, knowing that his first mission was accomplished. He didn't back down in the face of uncertainty. Oddly, he anticipated the next assignment. It was not enough to take the first lump sum of money and move out to get him a place; he had a plan. He needed to be as efficient and strategic as possible if he desired to reach his ultimate goals.

"Remember what I told you," the rasp in Calvin's voice had the ability to place fear in anyone's heart. He locked eyes with Samson, grabbing a hold of his bag; keeping him from fully exiting the vehicle. He nodded again and broke free of his hold.

"We're good!"

The building lay quiet, which had been expected at this hour of the night. He crept past the first unit in the apartment on her side of the hallway, hoping not to disturb Miss Jeanie, who managed to never sleep and stayed abreast of any and all activities in the building she deemed her own. She entitled herself the self-proclaimed "Neighborhood Watch Lady" with little to no input or support from the tenants in the building.

She periodically roamed down the hallway in her white and pink floral nightgown and purple bonnet, dragging her left foot across the hardwood floors in her cheetah print slippers, looking for anything she could stick her nose into. The truth is, she didn't have much business of her own to tend to, so she made do with the drama in the old building. She was well past her prime, widowed; with no interest in leaving the likes of her sweet home to build a new life after her husband's passing. If Samson had his guess, she was the walking dead. Her aging, frail body spoke tales of her neglecting to eat over catching the couple in Unit #3 argue, fuss and fight like cats and dogs as if it was her *One Life to Live*. If he could make it past her, all would be well. He could slip into his apartment and create a pallet on the floor to catch the few hours left in the night before sunrise.

"Little Boy... Excuse me... Little Boy," her screechy voice called out to him from the darkness of her doorway. Her dedication to the happenings of the neighborhood amazed him. The lights in her residence were all out. She peered at him through the crack of her wooden door. "I thought I heard someone creeping by." She tried to act like his steps startled her. "You look stressed. Are you all right? I just made a pot of coffee; you can come in and have some if you like." Her voice was ironically soothing to the sound. It was reminiscent of his paternal grandmother's, whom he rarely spent time with before she passed away. She waited for his response, as if she knew he had no other choice than to agree and join her.

As much as he knew he needed sleep, the fulfillment of that desire seemed impossible with all the scattered thoughts running through his brain.

*Who did I kill? Were they really dead? Am I protected? Why did I let myself do this? What if my father finds out?*

Coffee and a light conversation with Sherlock Holmes might be just what the doctor ordered. "Yes, ma'am, I guess I can take some." Despite his passion to be a thug, he knew how to respect his elders.

Although she welcomed a guest into her home, it lacked the presence of accepting visitors. Boxes, clothes and dust draped the chairs, tables and walls. She maneuvered through the dark room over to a single lamp propped on top of a broken coffee table, held up by a stack of tattered yellow pages. The one thing that appeared inviting was the coffee; the aroma filled the air, almost providing rejuvenation without consumption. "I've been watching you for the last few days. You haven't been around here very long." She started off subtle, but it was clear she had an agenda, placing the cup of coffee before him. "Are you courting that nice young girl down the hall or are you all just 'kicking it', like you young folks like to call it?" Her expression was priceless. She stared directly into his eyes, turning up her face, awaiting a response.

"She is helping me out for a few days. Nothing serious, just friends." He didn't feel like any of her questions warranted a response, but out of respect for the elderly, he answered. It was obvious she was lonely and needed some action in her life. Her home was dismal, like all the life evacuated with her late husband. A wedding picture of the two of them hung on the wall on her mantle as a reminder of the love once shared.

"Is that what they refer to it as now? Friends?" she didn't wait for a reply. She rattled on moving about the kitchen. "Back in my day, friends didn't spend too much time on top of each other unless they were going steady." The conversation became uncomfortable real quick. Samson had yet to add the sugar and cream to his coffee and she was already ready for him to spill the tea. It was clear to him that this old lady was out of her mind. The reality was, since being discovered by his father the night in the living room, he couldn't get as little as a smooch from his roommate, let alone sex. She never expected his parents to come home and find them in compromising positions. Edmond instantly pegged her as a whore and she was offended by it.

"Ma'am, I don't know what you are talking about and I am sure I don't want to discuss it either way with you. Thank you so much for your hospitality, but I think it is best if I take my coffee to go. I will return the cup later." The irritation was apparent in his voice and he made no gesture to hide it. The last thing he wanted to do was fall into the starring role of her late night stories. The one sip he had of the Folger's coffee was too good to leave behind, so he opted to do them both a favor and take it to go. He gradually made his way toward the door when she turned her back and ran out the door to freedom.

"It's late Sam. Where have you been?" his roommate instantly confronted him, frightened by the squeaking from the door hinges when he tiptoed in the door. Having to spend nights alone had her frustrated and a bit on edge.

"I was just out taking care of business, making money. I'll be outta here soon, so you don't have to worry about me." He still possessed an air of agitation from his encounter with the den mother.

"Why are you so annoyed with me? I was worried about you." His lack of consideration for her was a major concern. He barely shared anything with her. She knew that her decision to hold back from him would strain their relationship, but she hoped that he would get over himself and realize that her care for him reached beyond their physical intimacy. "You don't have to be nasty." She crumpled her face up at him, hoping for him to get a new attitude.

"You don't have to worry about me. I am a man and I will be fine! Plus, I got that heat now, so don't nobody want to see me in these streets." He pulled out his gun and pointed it toward the wall to prove to her he was not merely talking. The gleam in his eyes was unrecognizable and unwelcoming. He was now different to her. He possessed a ghostly demeanor. He aimed and cocked his head to the side, showing her he was skilled and was not afraid to use it. He was still mumbling to himself, speaking to someone who was not present.

"Sam," she hesitated, "I need you to be careful. There are people out here who really don't have any sense. These *fools* are not caring about the games you are playin'. They will kill you! Do you understand that?" Her voice cracked when she elevated her tone. She felt he didn't quite understand what he was getting himself into. His newfound "gangsta" would get him killed on any day.

"I am one of 'these *fools*' and I ain't scared of nuttin' or nobody. I've already put in work. You better know about it." He stepped toward her with mustered up aggression. The cockiness was beginning to overtake him to a place of no return. He poked out his chest more and lifted his head as he did when he encountered Calvin Rogers for the first time. He reached out for her hand, but she refused it. He tried yet again to caress her face. She swatted at his hand, stepping back to give her a clear distance from him.

"I don't have time for this nonsense! You really think I'm playin' wit you... I guess you will spend another day on the couch so you can figure this all out and think. And what's up with the coffee mug? It will be real hard to be taken seriously as a thug with a mug." She rolled her eyes, traveled back to her bedroom, and slammed the bedroom door, leaving him in the living room to play with his toy and anything else, for that matter.

Samson was not moved by her concern and shrugged it off, as though she was just experiencing that womanly time of the month. She often became extremely hostile and sensitive when on her menstrual cycle. He would have liked to attribute her lack of affection to that as well, but he knew better than that. He plopped down on the sofa bed and immediately dialed up his boy, Mike. With all the commotion of things, he had not had the opportunity to get with his boys and show off. Mike kept the streets occupied, hustling for his daily bread; so reaching him was the easiest in the crew because he didn't have to concern himself with office rules and regulations or policies.

Just as expected, he picked up on the first ring. "What's up, my boy?"

"I finally got that heat! Yo boy is right now." Samson adjusted his volume in order to keep her from popping back out of her room to get on his case. The fact that after their exchange he was still able to sleep on the couch left him grateful.

"What you mean? It's not safe out here fo' you. We never let you get down because we were looking out for you. Your parents are good people. You don't need this life."

"What?" Samson was shocked by Mike's sudden change of heart. "I got this! I've been runnin' these streets."

"Remember who you are talking to? I've known you since the third grade. You couldn't hurt a fly."

"Oh really? So would a Neighborhood King hurt a fly?"

"You rockin' with Calvin Rogers now?"

"Yep. He officially put me on tonight. Body count one."

"So that's the kind of work you are putting in?" His roommate demanded after overhearing his conversation, he was using her landline so she felt she had the right to listen in. He didn't notice she was standing behind him. Without offering him time to respond, she slapped Samson upside the back of his head, causing him to jolt forward. "You ain't gone be in my house messin' with them." She snatched up his clothes, the blankets, and tossed them out of the front door. In an uproar, she disconnected the line. "Get out!" she yelled, exhausted from all the lugging and tugging of his belongings.

"So, it's like that?"

"It's like that! I didn't get with you because I thought you might be a thug—I actually liked you." She left it at that and slammed the door in his face.

"Trick, please." Samson mumbled to himself. His ego was partially bruised; however, he would not let her kill his vibe. He heard his elderly stalker shuffling down the hallway, still peeping into business—that was not her own.

"Little Boy, you can stay the night with me if you like and we can go steady." The old lady called from down the hallway, cackling for all the neighbors to hear.

# Chapter 11

The caution and construction tape covered the glass entrance doors and surrounded the exterior of the building. The shop was closed for the day due to some much-needed upgrades that Raquel needed completed immediately. Finding time in her busy schedule always proved to be hectic; women constantly needed their hair weaves tightened and edges smoothed. Despite their grumbles and murmuring, clients were well informed ahead of time of the shop closure. For the most part, it created a daily soiree for the ladies of the community. She maintained the state-of-the-art equipment to keep the shop in its true elegance by periodically shutting down for maintenance. However, the closing of the salon presented the perfect opportunity to meet up with Calvin and discuss her son's behavior as of late. She was still unable to get a hold of him to calm him down and talk him off the ledge of going on a killing rampage. She didn't want him becoming the headline on the 10 o'clock news to increase the steadily growing homicide rate.

She did not raise a killer, and it was not his style. Charles had his occasional tantrums as a child, but generally, he was a very mild-tempered young man. He found himself in trouble, not on the account of his hot-tempered attitude, but due to his ability to stumble into mishaps and misfortune. He lived for drama and dysfunction. Almost as if all hell was not breaking loose around him, that the universe was somehow off scale and needed his assistance to keep itself balanced. He respected authority to a certain degree, but hated following rules. All his principals had Raquel's personal number on speed dial for every time he made a grand entrance into the principal's office. His love for drama is what attracted him to the bodyguard profession.

The first time he mentioned the idea of being a close protection officer to Raquel, she flipped out. Her only son could have found something a little less dangerous, but it was in his DNA. Although he found himself in trouble constantly as a minor; before the incident at the nightclub, he didn't have a record. He needed the sustained thrill of life, so naturally, being a bodyguard worked in his favor. He paid his dues as a security guard and worked diligently to be accepted into the police academy, which he eventually dropped out of due to irreconcilable differences. He used much of the training he did receive to start his own company, offering personal protection and high-level security for the upper echelon of the community. Yet, when he got in his own way, there was no stopping him and for Raquel, desperate times called for desperate measures.

There was a light tap on the glass door. *On time, as usual.* She waited a moment before heading towards the door to let him in. With a swift glimpse in the mirror, it graciously informed her that she was in need of a few touch ups herself. She gently pressed the curling iron across her edges, added a few curls where they had fallen, and applied a new layer of gloss to her lips to make sure they were shimmering and enticing. Despite the fact that she was no longer interested in Calvin, she still wanted him to desire her. It was definitely a turn on and an ego booster for her to watch men seductively scan her body from head to toe, drooling over her frame. Calvin happened to be a lips man, so if she wanted to make any progress with him, it was imperative that her best feature, in his opinion, was on point.

He knocked a few more times on the glass. God natured him to be a moderately patient man, unless it interfered with his moneymaking. He waited, knowing Raquel had no sense of urgency, especially when it came to him. Notwithstanding that he refused to settle down with Raquel in their younger years, he still cared about her. As a teenage boy, his priorities were not set on maintaining a long-term relationship. It was more-or-less set on having sex with as many attractive women as possible, while still dating her. He was immature when they dated, no different from any other boy his age at the time. Truth be told, Raquel was not Miss Faithful. She dibbled and dabbled in dirt of her own, but her hurt was not immune to the hurt he bestowed upon her and neither was his. Yet, even in their seasoned years of adulthood, their priorities remained the same.

When Calvin first met Raquel, times were different. He, being a few years older than her, saw her as mature for her age and much more developed and attractive than the other girls his age in and around the neighborhood. As an older boy with money in his pocket, he already had the advantage over the little boys that would attempt to court her. He was aware that young girls lived to brag to their girlfriends that they had a boyfriend that was out of school with a car. But Raquel was not that easy to woo. She was sassy. It was evident she knew what she was working with and promised herself that she would make him work for it.

Eventually, they began dating, and things were fun. He paid for everything and took her everywhere. At the time, he was in the midst of building his business and street credibility. As he made more money, he spent less time courting her. He heard from a few of his friends that she had been spending time with a boy from her school that was on the track team. He didn't pay it too much attention, because in his mind, this young boy could keep her occupied while he was handling his business. The words of his father always stayed with him "never let a woman come between you and your empire." When he needed or wanted to see her, she made herself available for him to slide through, and for him, that was enough. Unfortunately for her, it began to take its toll.

She began to spend more time with Edmond. Edmond made promises that he wouldn't treat her like Calvin did. He stepped up in ways she had never known a man to do and before she knew it—she had fallen. Yet, her adolescent heart still clung to the idea of Calvin, so when he called, she continued to make herself available to him, even behind Edmond's back. What he didn't know wouldn't hurt him, is what she convinced herself of. Over time, she wanted to come clean. Before she knew it, she had convinced herself it really didn't matter either way because she was only getting half of two men, which equaled one whole. It worked for her.

"What's up Mama? You look good!" Just as Raquel had hoped, he was plugged in to her. He grabbed her by her 30-inch waist and pulled her in close for a quick embrace. The gap of time that lapsed between the two of them seemed minimal, as it was only yesterday that they frolicked in the bond of lust. He appeared as if time stood motionless and decided that it refused to allow him to age.

*Damn, he looks good!* Raquel thought to herself. He still possessed the sex appeal that so easily got her caught up when they were teenagers. The fact that he was so confident, so sure of himself, so focused on business, even now turned her on. She turned away briefly to gain her composure, to hide her face, which always made her emotions obvious. She was beginning to lose sight of the reason that she had invited him to her workplace in the first place. *Think, think, think! Snap out of it!* He playfully slapped her butt to let her know he was still very much in control and had no animosity toward her. He had no reason to. He knew why she moved on, and he could not blame her. She giggled like a schoolgirl. His timing made it seem as though he was reading her inner thoughts.

"You better stop! I didn't call you here for that." She regained her composure to focus on the business at hand, took a seat in the VIP chair, and offered him a seat, which he refused. "Now Calvin…" It was best that she jump right into it before she lost her zest and zeal in the matter. "I try to leave you alone when it comes to Charles, since you gave up custody and have never really in no way, shape, form, or fashion been present as his father; however, things have gone too far. I can't help him anymore. I am all out of ideas and tricks up my sleeve. And I refuse to get Ed involved in this." She fought back the tears that were fighting to make their acquaintance. The thought of her only boy in trouble overwhelmed her.

"What is the issue, Rocky? I don't understand what you think I will be able to do. As you have so eloquently stated, I am not his daddy and I don't want anything to do with him. You were never even able to prove he was mine in the first place; but

114

when you are in trouble, he mysteriously becomes my son again." He replied nonchalantly. He spoke the truth even when he knew it might upset her.

"You practically know everybody in this town! Charles is trying to kill someone and I can't have my baby going to jail or, worse, getting killed. He is all I have. You gotta do something!" Ignoring everything he just said, she frantically ran over to her purse and snatched out all the bills she had from the clients she serviced the previous day, counting it out and throwing it in the air. "How much is it going to cost? I'll pay you."

"I don't need your money, Baby Doll. But there is something you can do for me?" He cocked his head to the side with a devious smile plastered across his face while he rubbed his graying goatee underneath his chin. He moved in closer to her, grabbing at her waist again. "You can give Big Daddy some of your sweetness. I mean, you are handing it out like candy on Halloween, anyway. Judge Frederick Price got a piece, right?" Her jaw dropped immediately and eyes widened in shame.

"How did you know about that?" She was dumbfounded. It was supposed to be their secret. Judge Price knew that no good would come from the uncovering of their agreement. Especially since he could lose his judge seat and never work again.

"It is my job to know everything that goes down in my city. I already took care of the problem, anyway. Just keep your damn legs closed, so I don't have to take out anybody else. Imagine I used to like Judge Price; he was one of the better-paid judges on my payroll. Just don't forget who taught you the game." He slapped her butt one last time with the intent of playful discipline.

"Mama, what the hell is this *son-of-a-bitch* Calvin doin' here?

115

I told yo' ass to stay away from me and my family." Through the intensity of the conversation, they failed to see Charles slip into the shop to catch the tail end of the conversation. He immediately reached for his back pocket to ensure his gun was in place.

"Pook! I don't need you to get upset. I called him here to talk," explaining as she ran over to him, ready to play defense against his attack. Raquel was aware that the two of them in the same vicinity would not fare a positive outcome if not handled correctly. Charles had not responded to her message to come and see her, so she figured he was out in the streets stirring up trouble.

"What the hell do you have to say to *him*, Mama?" Now addressing her directly. Charles was definitely on edge. It took every fiber to restrain himself from doing her company any harm. The hatred he had for Calvin was birthed years ago when he initially approached him about being down with his organization and refused. He did not agree with his business tactics and how he preyed upon the youth, filling their imaginations with hopes and dreams that he had no desire to fulfill.

"Calm, yo' ass down Charles Simmons! He is leaving," she demanded. Raquel reluctantly placed her hands upon his shoulders to grab him before he made any attempt to lunge at Calvin, who stood facing Charles, unaffected by his harsh language and tone.

"Oh, Baby Doll. Now you want me to leave? First, you want me to fix *his* problem and now when he shows up, you want me to leave. Well, I ain't ready to go yet. Have a seat son, let's all have a family reunion." His tone was patronizing.

"Mama, what the hell is he talking about? Fix my problem?"

Raquel was speechless. He slowed his speech to calm himself. He would give his mother the opportunity to offer a logical explanation, just in case she failed to hear him the first time he asked. "I'm gonna ask one more time… Why… the hell… is… he… here?" Charles sensed that certain things were not adding up. He seemed more disturbed by Calvin's presence than his mother did, and she knew the type of reputation he had around town. For all he knew, Calvin was attempting to get her caught up in some illegal business or after her for some reason. He figured he might be after his mom since he refused to be a part of the "Neighborhood Kings." No one was going to come into his space and threaten his family. It was his responsibility to keep the family protected.

"Rocky…" Calvin plopped down in the nearest styling chair and propped his leg up, finding this the perfect time to accept the seat that she previously offered him. "Please explain to the boy why I am here."

All eyes and attention were on Raquel. Charles was fuming; his eyes were deadlocked on her to avoid any interaction with Calvin. He tightened his fists to keep himself from reacting out of emotion, but he was equipped with his gun if he needed to use it. It was hard to keep his composure with so much hatred and anger inside of him. Hatred for Calvin as a man, anger for the man that killed his boy Elijah, and not knowing if the two had anything to with the other. Ultimately, he feared what he might do to anyone in his path and the impact it would have on his mother.

"Charles… son…" she fumbled with her words as she wrestled to get them out. It was important for her to say the right words, to explain it in the right way. It was so easy when he was a boy, when he was innocent, and the value of her words

117

carried a little weight. She was *Mommy* and the element of *Daddy* was irrelevant because the necessities of life were taken care of. He had male mentors, uncles, and teachers. In her world, the absence of his father was a non-issue. Edmond was his father for all she was concerned. The fact that he never knew Calvin to be his biological father remained water under the bridge that she would address when they crossed it. Until now, life patterned itself to never lead to the water. She started again, deciding to take a new angle, "Calvin is helping me with some work for the shop. I didn't want you to know about it because I didn't want you to worry. He knows some of the best contractors who are giving me a good deal." She could not bring herself to speak the truth. It was too much. He didn't deserve to find out this way.

"Well, well, well, now isn't this cute? The family is together again. *Reunited, and it feels so good,*" she sang; "Now I never thought I would walk in here and see this sight!" Charlene Tucker had impeccable timing and no shame. She let herself in, since no one was responding to her constant knocking. Lucky for her, the door was left unlocked. Instantly, she spotted Calvin and felt God was finally giving her the opportunity to get even with Raquel.

She couldn't resist being messy. Charlene trotted slowly through the shop, making an even bigger scene than had already been scripted. "Nice to see you, Calvin. I'm glad that you are finally stepping into your fatherly role so my husband can focus more on his own. You are ready to be a daddy now?" Calvin only smirked and stayed posted in the same position, cool, calm and collected. He knew it was a matter of moments before everything would unfold and he had a front-row seat.

"Mama, what the hell is going on? *Dammit!* Say something!"

Charles yelled in anguish, fighting back every buried emotion that so desperately wanted to surface.

Raquel couldn't speak. It was too difficult. There was no way to overturn all the lies. She could see it in his eyes that she had lost him. The truth didn't matter. She broke the bond of their trust, their unit. She collapsed to the floor, weeping profusely. She made it her responsibility to clean up his every mess and call him out on it, but she was incapable of being called out on her own.

"Mama, you don't get to cry. This is not your pain," he could no longer contain himself. He had reached his wit's end. "How about I don't even give a damn! I'm out!" He turned and stormed out the shop, shattering her glass door with the force of slamming it. Pieces of glass scattered about the front entrance, adding another project to the list of repairs.

"Are you happy now, you no good *bitch*?" Raquel immediately charged in her direction, turning her rage toward Charlene. She threw out her arms in an attempt to push her down. Charlene quickly jerked her body to the side, knowing she was off balance and Raquel fell face-forward to the floor. She popped up immediately and charged at her again, digging her nails into her skin. Charlene had her fair share of fights back in the day, channeled her inner ghetto, got a hold of a piece of her hair, and tossed her to the ground again.

"I am going to leave you two ladies to work this out. Rocky, it was good seeing you. Don't worry; I will take care of the door. It is the least I can do." Calvin tossed a wad of rolled one hundred-dollar bills to where she was sprawled on the floor, panting as if she had been in an UFC battle and let himself out.

"Rocky, I am not your enemy. I just came to get my hair done and happened to stumble upon the family feud. I did my part by staying silent all these years, but I know you and Edmond are still messing around. I should be attacking yo' ass, but I'm grown. I have to worry about my own now. I kept my kids away at your request. Your secret was my secret and for years, I suffered. Not anymore. But I can see that you are in no condition to do my hair, so can I reschedule for another time?" Charlene knew she was picking at an open wound. For years, she wanted to speak up, to have a say, but she remained silent until Edmond's actions gave her the license to let it all out.

Raquel just lay silent, in her shame, on the floor, awaiting Charlene to make her exit.

# Chapter 12

"Let me in." Lance released the button on the intercom for Darnise to buzz him into her unit. She stayed in the heart of West Oakland, Acorn District. From the hearsay of the many street myths that circulated the city, most people who were unfamiliar with Oakland or just *bougie* in nature rarely traveled to this particular part of town for fear of being killed. Lance was not afraid to travel anywhere. For the most part, he dated women in every nook and cranny of the city; West Oakland was not to be left from the list. He didn't discriminate. As a matter-of-fact, it was purposefully orchestrated, so if he had a need, he would be covered for all circumstances and situations. Women willingly entered into companionship with him, knowing that they were not going to have him solely to themselves; however, it rarely mattered to them. Time spent with Lance was far worth it in their eyes.

Darnise buzzed him in. Quickly he waved off Jamie Lynn to let her know he was good and was out of sight, safe in the confines of her abode.

Darnise had the front door left slightly ajar for him. She needed to hurry back to the kitchen to attend to her version of southern fried chicken that she was preparing for Lance in case he needed some food to settle his stomach. From the aroma in the apartment, it was clear that it was chicken, but the edible nature was still to be determined. Smoke filled the hallway leading up to the kitchen, proving her novice cooking ability.

The burnt smell from the previous batch that she let sit too long in the grease hit his nose upon entry. He parked his fatigued body down on the couch and rested his feet on the wooden coffee table. He didn't bother going into the kitchen after her for any formal greeting. His place to unwind was always on the couch when he entered her apartment; to catch the highlights of missed games on ESPN or staying abreast of the world news on CNN. Lance had a fluctuating schedule due to his work hours at the Oakland Airport and often missed major games and current events. He had enough seniority to work when he felt it was necessary. Yet, he still had to adhere to the crazy work hours with TSA.

"Babe, you want a beer or something?" Darnise kissed him on his forehead as she often did when he neglected to greet her, "I'm making some fried chicken and cornbread. You hungry?" She called out back to him as she hurried her way into the kitchen once again to check on her meal. It was important to her that he understood she had his back. Her cooking did not compare to that of Miss Lydia's; but she constantly tried her best to impress the both of them. It was obvious to everyone, even to Darnise, that Lydia did not care for the likes of her, but that didn't stop her from putting forth a valiant effort to measure up to a fraction of her standards.

"Nah, I'm straight. I just need to chill for a minute while I try to reach Charles. He hasn't been answering any of my calls." He scoured through his phones, looking for any sign of a missed call or text message that he could have possibly overlooked.

Darnise sashayed in, draped in one of his navy blue dress shirts left in her possession from a previous sleepover, batter and flour from her cornbread-making-attempt smeared on her face and fingertips. She offered her index finger with a hint of batter left on it to get Lance to lick clean, as he often did when he was in a better mood or just horny and trying to get her excited for some foreplay. He instantly backed away from her in irritation at her playful disposition. Tonight was different; he was in no mood for her tasteless batter and antics. He swatted her hand away from his face and kept searching through his phone.

"Do you even know what happened?" She blurted out in a bit of frustration at his rejection. She could tell he was not in the best state of mind, so she thought it best not to beat around the bush to get him talking. "I heard from *Mooch*, who is the cousin of one of the bartenders at the club, that they weren't even trying to kill Elijah. As a matter-of-fact, they were after Charles and when Elijah went to get the car, they sprayed it up thinking it was him," she reported. His expression lay blank.

"Who would have it out for Charles? He gets along with practically everybody in this town. All this ain't adding up." Lance shook his head in disbelief. Everything in him still wanted to breakdown, to shed tears for his fallen brother, but his pride wouldn't let him. The battered man inside of him refused to reveal himself.

"That's not even the end of it. I know Charles might think it was 'The Neighborhood Kings' based on everything that went down at his birthday party, but word on the street is, Calvin Rogers already put a bullet in the dude that got Elijah." She spewed out the words as if she was in casual conversation with one of her girlfriends on the phone for daily girl chat.

As Lance listened to her carry on, his body tightened up, sending unfamiliar chills through his body. He appeared extremely anxious, almost like his life and existence were slipping away. He stared hard at the wall as if contemplating some form of a takeover. Fear, anger, and pain loomed in his eyes. He spoke without initiation; "I need to get a hold of my boy, before he does something stupid, hell… before I do something stupid." He gathered his things that were scattered about her place to make his exit. He had to make moves; he couldn't just sit in the house and allow Charles to handle it on his own. Charles was a certified bodyguard, but that didn't mean he had the ability to take on the entire neighborhood.

"You not gonna find him tonight, plus the streets are real hot right now. Charles don't need both of his boys gone. Just stay the night with me. I can keep your mind off of all of that." Darnise hurried to the doorway to block him from leaving and turned on her sultry, seductive alter ego tugging at his arm. She guided him back toward the couch, pulling him down to her level and rubbing her hand across his heaving chest. Lance remembered just how catering she could be. It was hard for him to resist her at times because she was so persistent. His mama was right; her legs were always open to his beck and call. He often didn't even have to ask as she served herself up on a platter for him each and every opportunity she had. She slowly unbuttoned her shirt, exposing her leopard print bra to tease him a bit, and tossed it to the floor, displaying her matching underwear. Then she slowly lifted his shirt, revealing his geometrically chiseled six-pack, pulling it up to his chest without his guided assistance and repositioned herself to maneuver on top of him, placing gentle kisses on his bare skin in a downward motion. She paused when she reached his waistline to unfasten his belt.

"Darnise, I'm not in the mood for this," he uttered with aggravation. She crumpled up her face in disbelief, knowing that he loved when she took control. That was the last thing she expected to hear from him, considering he accepted her invitation, knowing what she ultimately wanted. He pulled his shirt back down and scooted her off of him to the side. He never refused her before, so Darnise was unsure how to take it. She moved back toward him, hoping he was playing. Most of the time, he enjoyed her aggressive nature; she pressed forward. Again, he pushed her back, this time with a little more force. She instantly copped an attitude.

"Is it because of that stank ho' from the club?" She quickly reached for her shirt that had landed behind the couch and re-dressed herself. The incident from the club immediately came to her remembrance; it was the easiest way for her to get back at him. She had not forgotten; it just fell on the agenda for later on in the evening after her sexual appetite was curbed. Since he threw a wrench into her plan, it was the best time to bring it to the forefront for discussion.

"I'm just not in the mood. Stop trippin'. You shouldn't even be using that kind of language. It's not ladylike," Lance responded, patronizing her. He reached out for her bare thigh that lay across his legs to rub her into submission. She snatched her leg back and sat up to gain a good position on the couch for her rebuttal.

"It has never been a problem before. All of a sudden, this new *ho'* comes into your life and now you are a saint? I call B.S.! I'm gonna let you slide tonight because I know you are goin' thru' but please believe we will finish this later." Although she wanted him badly, she knew that his mental state was altered, and that it had nothing to do with her. When the time was right, she would make sure to finish the conversation. Darnise rarely forgot a thing. She could bring up old incidents from months ago with full recollection of all details of what was said, who was involved, and what they had on. She ungrudgingly removed herself and whisked away to the kitchen to package up the uneaten food. She retired to her bedroom with her vibrator, that would not deny her company.

The continuous sound of loud banging on the front door startled her out of her sleep. Lance, oblivious to the loud noise coming from outside, stayed sprawled out across the sofa bed, dormant at the commotion. After their little spat, Darnise locked herself in her bedroom to pleasure herself while Lance dozed off on the couch. She thought it best to let him sleep to avoid him being restless in the morning. She had her qualms with him, but despite it all, she loved him and truly had his back. When she wasn't slashing his tires, burning his clothes or picking fights with the women she caught him messing around with; she was his ride-or-die-chick. She invested so many years into their relationship that sooner or later he would be bound to commit to her fully and stop with all the childish games. It was her fault for falling for him, knowing he was not in a place of desiring commitment.

Although Darnise spent more than your average amount of time basking in "hood" behaviors; she was an intelligent girl. Educated through the public school system, she went on to graduate with her bachelor's degree from San Jose State. At twenty-five years of age, she didn't have any children, but hopes of every little girl's dream of the white picket fence fantasy. When she was sixteen years old, she got pregnant by one of the older boys who lived in her building growing up. Once her mama got wind of it, she forced her to get an abortion, refusing to allow another mouth to feed put them out in the streets. Life was difficult enough with her mom and two siblings living out of government housing and watching her mother's on-again-off-again boyfriend come home and take out his life's frustrations on her mother. She made do. She worked on weekends at the local mini-mart and deli to help bring in extra cash and kept money on the side to keep her hair styled and her nails manicured.

When she met Lance one night at the club, she felt she hit the jackpot. He was handsome, athletic, and popular around town, which meant he had "instant access," and he had a great personality. She was instantly mesmerized by his charm and ate up all of his game. Her sass is what drew him in to her. He liked a girl with a bit of spice, who knew how to hold herself and her man down. He rocked with her because she was real, even with the occasional sew-in weave and fake lashes. As long as when she stepped out of the house, she was red carpet ready; he didn't mind how she got there.

Darnise heard the knocking first and hurried to the living room, where he lay sprawled across the couch in his boxers and shook Lance out of his sleep.

"Open up! It's the police. Lance Brown, we have a warrant for your arrest." The knocking persisted. "We know you are in there. Darnise Jacobs, please cooperate with us and open the door."

Darnise looked over to Lance for approval to let the knocking guest in. Lance scrambled around the living room, locating his pants and his shirt to throw on before opening the door, still trying to gain his bearings. He signaled to her to give them a response, to keep her door from being smashed in.

"Okay. One moment. Let me throw on some clothes." She looked at Lance for some answers and assurance that if she opened the door, she would be able to see him again. He was clueless. He knew at this point that it could be anyone.

He signaled to instruct her to open the door. A tall, white, middle-aged man stood at the door with his partner a few feet behind on high alert if he decided to try anything tricky. "Lance Brown, sorry to disturb you this early in the morning, but we have a warrant out for your arrest for the rape of Tanisha Watkins. We have to bring you down to the station for some questioning." The officer was not abrasive. He appeared strangely amiable, only doing the job he was called to do, so Lance decided to cooperate. He had no more fight left in him. For all he knew, he was being arrested for the altercation at the diner or, at worst, for something Charles did.

It didn't dawn on Lance that he was being arrested for rape until the officer began to place the handcuffs around his wrists, patting him down in search of contraband and concealed weapons. His manhood was violated with each grab and tug. He was helpless. Even though this time they didn't use the force as the officers applied when he was in the diner.

"Rape! I didn't even touch that girl!" he pleaded as the officer handcuffed him while reading and reminding him of his Miranda rights. "Babe, call my mama to get my lawyer down to the police station." Darnise didn't budge. She stared back at him with no expression.

She held her stance, confused as to which part she was to play in this situation. He had refused her the night before and took every opportunity to step out on her with anything with legs and breasts. Now he found himself in a serious predicament. The man she knew and had grown to love wouldn't take advantage of a woman. He surely never had to with her. He was so warm and charming. Any woman would kill for the chance to be wrapped up in his embrace. However, things were different now; he was cold toward her. He refused her touch—her love. Her thoughts abruptly took a change in course. *Maybe it is something I failed to do.* She thought to herself, wondering if she had been a little more persistent in getting him back or keeping him on lockdown that this may not have occurred.

The short, uncomfortable, confined ride down to the station allowed no time for Lance to even wrap his head around the situation, yet the bars on the windows gave the impression he was already guilty. He nearly dodged an arrest the night before and turned around to find himself arrested, anyway. He laid his head back on the hard plastic seat that provided minimal comfort. Through the bumps and turns of the police vehicle, all he could think about was Jamie Lynn. She supported him when she had yet to know the man he truly knew himself to be; and Darnise, the lady he abandoned her to be with, stood inaudible, motionless, making all of her claims of love and support appear false in his eyesight.

The arresting officer spoke very few words to him during the ride, as if he could hear his thoughts, and decided to give reverence to his stream of consciousness. The black wrought-iron gate rolled back to let them in. Lance swallowed hard and took a strong breath in, as in ritual; to brace him for what was to come. He wriggled his way out of the car, with no assistance from the officer, placing his feet firmly against the concrete to gain his balance.

The booking room welcomed his presence with open arms; there was definitely no shortage of young black males to co-exist with him for the duration of his stay. This would be his first dance with the booking process. He had been arrested before, but somehow never made it down to the station. He feared what lingered on the inside. He had heard stories and prided himself on the clean reputation, but this was serious; he could lose his freedom behind this. The photograph, fingerprinting and stripping of his dignity made way to manifest consent to the allegations against him.

They guided him through the lifeless hallway, surrounded by white walls and judgmental eyes. The investigator joined Lance in room 3; he was a large, slightly balding Black man, who seemed to have had his fair share of breakfast, lunch and dinner. His all-white mustache was sprinkled with crumbs from his after-breakfast snack. He sipped his coffee before placing it down on the small table that was flush against the wall that held the secret mirror Lance remembered seeing in all the crime investigation shows. The chair left empty gave him the sense that someone else was soon to join the affair.

"These White people keep this station so cold, they know Black people like it hot!" The investigator chuckled, finally breaking the silence, coughing uncontrollably through his laughter. It was obvious that he had been at the station some time, since he was blatantly calling out his white comrades that were surely listening through the two-way mirror. "Trust me, I don't like doing this, but I got to." He became serious, as if now he was ready to get down to business. "I presume that the officer has already read you your rights, but just in case he failed to do so, I am going to explain them and have you to sign this document."

130

He paused a moment to ensure Lance understood the directions and proceeded. Lance nodded in agreement to the given instructions. "You have the right to remain silent. You do not have to speak with us. If you do decide to speak with us, anything that you say can and will be used against you in court. You have the right to talk to a lawyer before you talk to us. The lawyer can be here with you before we ask you questions or during the entire time we ask you questions." With the reading of every right, beads of sweat began to form on the top of Lance's head. The ice-cooling air from the air-conditioned room dissipated and a feeling of extreme warmth overtook his body. "If you cannot afford a lawyer, one will be provided for you, free of charge, and you can stop answering questions at any time you want. If you understand each one, I need you to initial each line and sign at the bottom of the document." Lance signed, anxious to get the interrogation process started, in order to get back home. He noticed the audio light was not turned on, which made him slightly concerned.

Two taps on the door alerted them that his lawyer had arrived. Darnise made the call, after all. Mr. Fleming had impeccable timing. Since he had successfully assisted Charles in his case, Lance kept his contact information just in case he needed it, but truly prayed that he would never use it. Mr. Fleming greeted his client and focused directly on the business at hand. "Why was my client arrested and what is he being charged for?" He questioned, very stern, not breaking his eye contact with the old Black man.

He cleared his throat for the fifth time since entering the room. "Rape. We have probable cause that your client was involved in the sexual assault of Tanisha Watkins."

"Rape!" Lance blurted out unconsciously, as if it was the first

131

time he had heard the allegation. After all that had transpired, it was finally beginning to settle in.

"Yes Mr. Brown, Rape. You know, the non-consensual sexual intercourse that takes place between two or more individuals by imposing physical force, threat of injury or other duress." The elderly, staid officer had finished his second cup of coffee and was on a roll. "She filed a report against you in our office. Now when was the last time you saw Ms. Watkins?"

Lance looked over at Mr. Fleming for permission to speak. He nodded to let him know it was safe to do so, but he winced at him to proceed with caution. Mr. Fleming felt it unnecessary to keep him from exposing his truth. He was confident in his innocence. Everything about his body language that he learned in law school defined his irreproachability.

"I saw her the other day; when she came to my mama's house."

"And what happened?"

"She was upset, as usual, and doing everything in her power to get back with me. We argued a bit, and she told me she was pregnant. We exchanged some choice words, and she tried to attack me. I apprehended her, and then she left. She was talking crazy, but I didn't rape her."

"Now, we are doing most of this for the formalities. In most cases, the District Attorney will drop a rape charge if they think they cannot prove the charge beyond a reasonable doubt." The investigator was oddly thorough in his explanations. Lance just shrugged it off as normal protocol and continued to listen. "They can use two different tools to determine whether they should prosecute: a polygraph or a sexual assault nurse examination. A SANE is an examination of the alleged victim's body for evidence by a trained nurse to identify vaginal bruising." He seemed so matter-of-fact with his statements, yet unbothered by the process, which made Lance even more nervous. "If she refuses to participate in the determining tools, then we will be forced to drop the charges." With his next statement, things became extremely weird. "We have reason to believe that she will not proceed with this investigation."

Lance glanced over to the audio light, which remained in the off position. "Excuse me, sir, but I don't seem to understand what's going on. I was picked up from my home on some rape charges and now you are telling me it was all for nothing? This doesn't make any damn sense!"

"Not exactly." The investigator shifted in his seat and in ritual cleared his throat. "There is another ongoing investigation. As I shared in the beginning, I have to go through the formalities. The brother of the alleged victim was found dead. We have reason to believe she had him to come after you in retaliation for the altercation you described that transpired outside of your mother's house. We have written statements from neighbors about what happened, so your story checks out. But we have a bigger problem."

Mr. Fleming sat with his legs crossed, tuned in to what the man was sharing, almost as if he was at home watching an episode of "The First 48". The investigator continued. "We need to know your involvement with this homicide. If you notice, the audio recording is turned off. No one is behind the mirror. It is just you and me, and your lawyer, of course. Just two Black men shooting the breeze." He leaned back in his chair and propped his feet up on the table next to his empty coffee mug, crossing his arms across his chest and protruding belly.

"I didn't kill nobody," Lance insisted.

"What is your relationship with Elijah Naples?"

"He was one of my best friends."

"So you mean to tell me that one of your best friends was shot in cold blood and you didn't go after his assassin?" The investigator dropped his feet down and leaned into Lance, not far from his face, giving Lance an up close and personal whiff of his coffee breath.

"I ain't got nothin' to do with that. I didn't kill nobody."

"What happened at the 24-hour diner?" He leaned back into his original position.

"I got upset when I heard the news about Elijah and had a breakdown."

"Who is Jamie-Lynn Johnson? Does she know about Darnise Jacobs?"

The flood of questions began to upset him. "I'm sorry; sir, but I don't see how any of this has to do with the other. Mr. Fleming, I am ready to get out of here. If I am not being charged with anything, then I am free to go, right?" Lance rose up from his seat, preparing to make his exit.

"That is correct, but I think you may want to hear me out before you run out of here with no protection."

"Protection? What the hell do I need protection from?" He turned to square up with the investigator, who was still seated in his relaxed position.

"First of all, from yourself. Second, from the thugs who might be after you in retaliation for the killing of their own. Here are the facts: There was an altercation at Sweets Ballroom in celebration of your best friend's birthday, then Ms. Watkins accused you of raping her, who was identified as a patron at Sweets that night. Next, there is an altercation at The Shadow Bar in which you are seen fleeing the scene with Ms. Johnson. Next, we receive a call that Elijah Naples, your best friend, had been murdered. Charles Simmons goes missing. Tony Watkins, Tanisha's older brother, is found murdered in an alley. When it is time to bring you in for questioning, you are now conveniently in Ms. Jacobs' home. How does that sound to you?"

"With all due respect, do you have a gun with my prints? Was my blood found at the crime scene? Am I still under arrest? If the answer remains 'No', then I'm outta here."

Finally released from his trance, Mr. Fleming decided to add his two cents. "My client is correct. If there are no charges held against my client, then he is free to go."

The investigator shook his head in disbelief as if he knew something that they did not and leaving would turn up in tragedy. He waved them off, allowing Lance and his lawyer to exit the room. As soon as they were cleared from the room, the investigator picked up his cell and dialed, "Make sure the boy is protected," he immediately hung up the phone and stared blankly at the mirror.

# Chapter 13

"Happy Anniversary Baby." Edmond pronounced, holding one long stem rose and a box of See's candy as Charlene crossed the threshold leading into the foyer of their home. Praying to God her reaction would be pleasant.

He laid pink rose petals to cover the entrance to surprise her upon walking through the door. Edmond stayed up late the night before topping off his spectacular anniversary surprise for his wife, pealing each rose petal from the stem, soaking them in jasmine to provide the perfect aroma. He envisioned that once she arrived home from her hair appointment, she would follow the trail of rose petals to the master bathroom, where Edmond had prepared a rose petal bubble bath with candles and soft jazz music serenading in the background. He would towel dry her entire body and escort her into their bedroom, where he hand-picked her wardrobe for their evening to go out on the town in San Francisco, complete with dinner, dancing and a horse and carriage ride on the pier.

What really happened was slightly different.

Edmond perused Charlene; examining her from head to toe, trying to make sense of the fact that she looked very similar to the way she looked when she left the house that morning. Her hair remained wrapped in the silk scarf wrap she frequently wore when heading to the hair salon. She pushed past his pitiful attempt to patchwork their relationship, huffing and puffing under her breath. She was unmoved by the rose petal layout that he crafted out of his love and dedication to sustain their marriage.

"What is the problem, Charlene? Did you say something to Raquel? This is supposed to be our special day." He gave her another thorough look over, shaking his head in disbelief.

She paced back and forth, still uttering words under her breath, asking herself questions she had no intention of answering. Clearly making a scene, even if no one was present to witness it. "Oh, I said something alright." She pulled back her head and wriggled her finger in his face.

"Baby, we talked about this. You know you weren't supposed to say anything."

"Do you even want to know what happened, or are you going to just blame me? I'm not taking the blame for this one. Not after all we have been through. I'm done fighting these damn skeletons. I'm free, Ed. I'm finally free, baby!" She continued her pacing, throwing her hands up in the air to illustrate her newfound freedom. She would not allow him to get a word in or alter her mood.

"What are you talking about? Just tell me what happened and why I paid all that money for you to come back here looking the same way you left *and* with a bad attitude?"

"I ran into Raquel and Calvin at the salon today. I show up ready to get my hair done, knocked on the door and no one answered. I let myself in and lo-and-behold, there are Raquel and Calvin arguing about you! And guess what? Charles was there too, lost and confused about everything. That boy still doesn't know Calvin is his real daddy. So I told him!"

"You did what?" Edmond finally dropped the contents to the floor that he'd been holding since she entered. He took a step closer to her to get the full explanation of how all of this really went down. He made sure, though, to maintain a steady distance, so he couldn't make any sudden movements that could turn the situation sour.

"I didn't exactly say it, but I implied it." She stepped back and softened her tone. "It is time you do right by your own family and stop running to Raquel Simmons' every cry for help. Our kids are not little anymore. There's nothing more to hide, Edmond," she reasoned in an attempt to justify her actions to him. Charlene took a step closer, reached out to grab his hand, but he refused it.

"You knew what the situation was before we even married. This is not the first time something like this has happened and you stayed in your place before. The majority of this mess was your idea, anyway."

"Ed. Let's not go there because then we will have to bring up the past and I don't think you want to do that. We let a lot of the mess go years ago. You... Raquel... Calvin. We let that go, right, babe? We let that go, right babe?" she repeated herself, hoping for a favorable response. She needed him to come clean about his infidelity. She willingly allowed his cheating in the past, but they had grown to a point in their marriage where he vowed to do right by her and steer clear of stepping out on her. "You ain't been with her, right babe?" she gritted her teeth together and eased out her question one final time.

The sound of footsteps on the porch stifled them from their heated discussion. Samson decided that using the doorbell would be meaningless with all the yelling he heard coming from the house. Instead, he opted to bang on the iron security gate that had an automatic lock to keep out unwanted visitors. Samson used the payphone during his night on the streets and informed his mother that he was ready to come home. He wanted to try to mend things with his father since the living arrangements he had fallen apart.

The house seemed a little different, a feeling of frigidness. He could sense it. The familial love and joy that the home carried when he was a child had gone away. Debra was away at school and Edmond and Charlene were constantly bickering. In a way, he sensed that his feud with his father kept his parents at odds. He didn't desire for them to quarrel due to his mistakes. He had to take some ownership of the situation and make it right.

He waited for one of them to notice the banging and acknowledge his presence.

Charlene pushed back the curtains and peeked out the window, avoiding the peephole affixed to the door. "Good. Samson is here. Let's start by telling him the truth. I think he deserves to hear it straight from his father." Charlene pranced over to the door to let him in, relieved that she now had a little backup.

She greeted her baby with a tight embrace. It had been days since she last saw him; for her, it felt like an eternity. She released him and shot an uneasy glance at Edmond, hoping he would follow suit. Edmond barely made eye contact with her or him, for that matter; still clinging to a piece of the dissatisfaction he had for his actions and his lifestyle choices. For Edmond, life did not need to be difficult for Samson. He had two able-bodied parents who provided everything he could ever possibly need in life. His life choices were simple, but he chose to go out in the streets and hustle as if it were his only option.

Edmond was disinclined to reveal his truth, because his truth could tear the family apart. He had held on to it for so long; it almost wasn't worth the headache, but Charlene was right. He was of age. It was time for him to understand their family dynamic; much of what cultivated Samson came straight from Edmond. He was a chip off the old block and the apple really didn't fall far from the tree. He motioned for Samson to take a seat on the sofa.

Edmond sat, making himself comfortable in his recliner. "Listen son, I haven't been completely honest with you and your sister *or* your mother, for that matter." He glanced over at Charlene to confirm if this was what she really wanted. She nodded in approval, eager to hear what he had to say.

"Wait. Pops, if you are going to tell me that you are really a woman, I don't want to hear that," Samson joked to breakdown the stiffness in the air. He knew that was the best way to reconcile with his father, plus the atmosphere was too serious for his nerves.

"Boy! I'll kill you!" He playfully popped the side of his head. "You know good and well, my stroke is too good to be a woman!" He thrust his pelvis in a slow upward motion, causing Charlene to blush in embarrassment at her husband's childish antics.

"Now that the two of you have officially made up, you can get back on topic. This is serious," Charlene interrupted, hoping to get to the good part about what he had been dishonest with her about.

"Your mother is right. As I was saying before, I have not been completely honest. Before you were born. I used to run the streets, very similar to how you are now. A lady by the name of Raquel Simmons, that I was dating, got pregnant. As her man, I felt it was my responsibility to step up to the plate to take care of it, so I did. I didn't realize that she had an on-again, off-again relationship with the infamous Calvin Rogers at the time." Hearing Calvin's name made Samson perk up a bit. He didn't want to give his connection to him away by making any sudden movements; so he pretended to cough in his hands, so his father would not stop talking and continue.

Edmond gave Samson a moment to clear his throat and continued; "I knew she did her thang when I wasn't around, but I didn't make it my business to care who she was with. I found out three years later that the son I had grown to love as my own was not mine. One day I was out with your mother and Calvin came and approached me with a proposition. I was in between jobs at the time, and he knew I had a relationship with Raquel. He informed me about a position with NUMMI that if I applied, it would be mine and I would work in conjunction with him on a few things, in return for raising Charles, since he wanted no part in his life."

Edmond sat quietly for a moment and thought about his words. He closed his eyes in an effort to hide the torment he was carrying with this secret. Tears began to form in the corner of his eyes. He thought about the fact that Calvin willingly gave up the opportunity to be a part of his son's life because he was too busy building his business and a son was not a part of the plan. He thought about how he had abandoned Raquel at the most vulnerable time of her life, because he was too hurt to deal with her and offer her his forgiveness. He thought about the fact that he put Charlene through agony some nights wondering where he was and if he would return, as he found refuge in different women who were able to satisfy his needs at that moment. He thought about how Samson was lost just like he was and could fall victim to gun violence or drugs at any time at the rate he was going. He thought about his little girl that felt she had to give up her body to fit in and was suffering the loss of a baby as a result. He thought about how he ultimately failed at his responsibility to protect his family. He opened his eyes, gazed off at the ceiling, took in a deep breath, and continued.

"I accepted the offer. I needed the money, and I wanted to be in Charles' life any way I could. Your mother allowed this agreement to happen only if I stopped messing around with Raquel, which I did initially." He stole a quick glance at Charlene, who shook her head. She knew he had been unfaithful. He could not help himself. It had been part of the very thing that made him attractive to her. All the ladies desired him. She couldn't even be hurt by it. She was already numb to the pain. He shifted his attention back to Samson and continued, "I worked my way up in the company doing favors for Calvin here and there. Shipping cars with drugs, providing cars for various jobs, bodywork when necessary. When the company was getting ready to go under, my name and reputation were on the line and the government was going to conduct an investigation. Calvin came through in the midnight hour and kept the company alive through his relationships with some of the business owners, but eventually I knew I would have to repay him."

"Wait… wait… wait… Are you telling me that *you* work for Calvin Rogers?" Samson questioned, still piecing the story together.

"I'm telling you that I am not proud of what I have done and who I am. I made some mistakes along the way and I don't want you to make any like I made. That is why I offered you a position with the company. I did all the dirt. Everything is legit now, and it could all be yours." Samson fidgeted with his hands, contemplating revealing his own truth. *What's the worst that could happen?* He thought to himself.

"So I sort of have an older brother?" he asked, still feeling his way through his thoughts about his father's confession.

"Not exactly. He doesn't know about any of this, or you and Debra. He calls me 'Pops' and knows that I have been around, but he doesn't know his biological father. For all he knows, he left out of his life when he was a baby. We thought it best for him not to know. For all of you to be kept out of the situation." Charlene rushed over to Edmond and placed her arm around his waist. Talking about this particular subject caused her to be extra supportive. She was aware that the circumstances of the situation were difficult for Edmond and, although they had their fair share of marital spats; she was all in when it came to her husband and children.

"Dad, I have something to tell you?" The energy in the room shifted toward Samson.

"Samson, what is going on? Please don't tell me you got someone pregnant?" Charlene asked, concerned; preparing to have a breakdown if her assumptions were true. She rubbed Edmond's back, still managing to console him, but more so to keep her own emotions intact.

"I met Calvin Rogers the other day, and I have been working for him." He stated in a low tone, then lowering his head.

"You did what? Do you know what kind of mess you are into?" Edmond became livid. He took a step closer toward him and gently removed Charlene's hand from his back.

"I know… I know… he told me that you were old friends… and… and," he stopped mid-sentence, then blurted out, "I shot someone… I killed him."

"Who the hell did you kill?" Edmond demanded. "Old friends? Boy, you better get to explanin'. What you are sayin' is not adding up."

"I don't know… I don't know… some local drug dealer who tried to cross Calvin; I guess… I didn't ask no questions." Samson had trouble getting a handle on his confession. He didn't fully prepare for the words to be released in that manner. In his mind, he knew a confession was good for the soul. However, the reality of the matter was that his confession was digging a deeper ditch for his own demise; that he may not have the ability to crawl his way out of alive.

At his words, Charlene jumped up and grabbed him where he sat and violently shook him. "Who? Who did you kill? *Not my baby. This is not happening. My son is not a killer.* How did you get mixed up with Calvin?" She turned in outrage to Edmond. "Ed, you better fix this. All these years, this has been looming over our heads. This man is trying to take from you what he never had. Fix this now!" Her anger was overtaking her. Her entire body trembled. All of it was too much to handle. "If you don't take care of this, dammit, I will!" She raced over to her purse to retrieve her cell phone to call Debra. She was hysterical. She ravaged through her oversize bag, tossing out items. It seemed as though everything lay in the way. Her plan was to get Debra on the next flight back to Oakland. For such a time as this, she needed her family together.

"Hi Mama. Is something wrong? You don't sound OK."

"I am making arrangements for you to come home on the

next flight to Oakland. Your father wants to see you. Pack your bags." She didn't leave time for an explanation and hung up the phone to look up the next available flight she could purchase to get her daughter back home. When her mother was frantic like that, Debra knew it best to not ask any questions and be obedient. They were in a better place now since patching things up in the hospital and with their newfound friendship; she hoped to keep it that way.

# Chapter 14

As soon as my mother rang my phone, I knew something serious had been going on. I could recognize something different in her voice, in her demeanor. First of all, she did not like to spend money when she felt it was unnecessary. I wouldn't go as far as calling her and my father cheap, but they were definitely knocking on *Cheap's* doorstep trying to maintain their lifelong membership. She already made two trips to Riverside, which she made sure to remind me of the duration of her visit. If I had a job, I would have purchased the ticket myself to save myself from the headache of her tirade. However, I didn't have a dime to my name, so unfortunately that meant I was at her will.

"Hey Deb. Is everything all right?" My roommate finally decided to make her grand entrance and come home, slinging her bags on the couch and floor from days of being away.

"Gurrrl, if you only knew," I replied, placing the phone down to give her my undivided attention. In addition to working, she had spent some time at her boyfriend's house because it was closer to her job and, quite frankly, she wanted to be close to him and I couldn't blame her. He had his own place and money to take care of both of them. Who would turn that down?

"I'm sorry I have been M.I.A., but you know how it goes. I had to see my beau;" she smiled and did a quick white girl version of the back roll dance to let me know just how she had been getting down while she was away. "I did get your messages. Tell me what happened." She scurried over to the other side of the couch and plopped down on a pillow, since her luggage occupied the last available space on the opposite end. "Spit it out... what happened? Are you OK?" nudging me to get answers.

I knew the stream of questions would begin. Sarah Wiseman prided herself on being inquisitive and she would not stop until I answered. "You remember when you talked me into taking the pregnancy test?" Her eyes were glued on me as she listened.

"Yes, girl, yes... Are you preggo?" She leaned in and placed her hand on my leg, insisting that I answer as quickly as possible; the anticipation was killing her.

"Well...." I paused a moment of intensity. Plus, she failed to respond to my messages, so she obviously had been too preoccupied to find out sooner. I made her wait. I needed her to suffer a bit.

"Are you pregnant or not? Did you get the plus or the minus?" Her impatience had escalated to the next level of already being too anxious.

"Well... I was."

"What do you mean, you was?" She mimicked the exact words I used with uncertainty of where this conversation was going.

"The night I called you, I had a miscarriage." She gasped when the words released from my lips. "I was rushed to the hospital because I was having pains and bleeding."

She interrupted yet again, "Are you OK? Well, I see you are OK, but what happened? I'm sorry I couldn't be here when you needed me." She began to panic. She rose from her seat and wrapped her arms around me, hugging my waist and apologizing profusely.

I couldn't help the feeling that came over me. Tears emerged without warning. I realized that I had not dealt with the pain of losing the baby. I had not really given it too much thought with everything that happened with my mother and father. Through sobs, I managed to respond to her, "No. I'm not all right. I lost my baby Sarah! I barely knew I was pregnant and just like that, I lost my baby." She sensed I was having a hard time dealing with it. Beyond the tears, she connected with my abandonment.

"I'm a terrible friend. I wasn't here for you! I'm sorry!" Sarah couldn't help herself. She cried with me. She cleared her throat and wiped the lingering tear off her cheek. "I hate to spring this on you now, considering the situation, but I'm moving out." Her statement caught me off-guard. I felt as though we hadn't yet finished our talk. It was my moment of mourning and she was off to the races on a new topic of interest.

"Moving out? What do you mean? The school year just started. Where are you going?"

"I'm moving in with my boyfriend. We are going to get married."

"*Married*?" I couldn't believe the words that were coming out of her mouth. She had just made nineteen years of age and marriage didn't seem logical since she had just begun her studies. I understood, though, she was young and in love, at least for the moment. Her father did not tolerate her dating— just like my dad. She waited until she went away to college to even inform her parents that she had a boyfriend. They had been dating since middle school. It pained her to have to keep it a secret from them for so long, but she had no other choice.

"I think it is time. He told me he loved me and didn't want to live without me. He doesn't have the money right now for a ring, but we will just live together until our finances are all the way right. It's enough for me that he is keeping a steady shelter over my head."

"Sarah, do you hear yourself? You are not ready for this. Granted, he gets money from his parents, but you don't know the first thing about being on your own."

"And I guess because you are so experienced in life, you have all the answers? Huh? You don't know. He loves me!" She demanded in an attempt to convince me, but more importantly, herself.

"I don't want you to get the wrong idea; I just don't want you to get hurt moving too fast. Men can be wishy-washy. One day, he might wake up and not want you anymore; then you are left to pick up all the broken pieces of your heart that he let shatter right before your eyes."

"That would never happen with Brad. He loves me and we are getting married." Her face reddened and silent tears rolled down her face. I couldn't help but sense that something more was going on. She buried her head in her hands. "I don't have any other choice. I have herpes. I got it from him. No one else will ever want me or him for that matter, so we decided to stay together and get married and work through it."

"Are you crazy? That is the dumbest reason for getting married." I hated to have to be so blunt with her, but I couldn't stand her sequence of thought.

"What else am I supposed to do? I really do love him," she

cried out in desperation. The side arm of the chair now soaked with her tears. "My life is falling apart. And it's all my fault."

The conversation took a U-turn right under my nose and became about her and her situation. I thought that she wanted to console me and help me with my predicament, but I was wrong. She needed my shoulder just as much as I needed hers. The tragedy before us left us both lost and confused. I had no words for her; how could I? I recently learned that my mother willingly played the role as the side chick and my father had been deliberately unfaithful. My judgment was flawed. I should be right along with her throwing myself a pity-party. I lost a baby, but with everything occurring, I still saw it as a blessing in disguise. I truly believe the Good Lord was shielding me from hurt; that I had yet to experience.

"Sarah," I hesitated, "I don't know what to tell you. Believe me, I am in no place to pass judgment. I'm scared for you, for me. Just make sure you are ready. Call your father and tell him. I know it will break his heart to find out later." It was almost like my words fell on deaf ears; she just stared back at me with dismay.

My cell chimed with a text notification.

*Flight time 6:55am on Southwest at Ontario International Airport*

My mother did just as she said she would. I hurried and threw all I could find into a suitcase so I could call a cab and make it to the airport on time for the flight. It was clear that I was not going to get much sleep tonight. I felt bad having to leave Sarah alone after she confided in me about her situation, but she was a big girl and could handle it. Besides, she had not been there for me and had the audacity to leave me with the lease. I felt as though she had no intention of staying if I really needed her to do so.

After throwing all the unnecessary items into my suitcase, it became time for my grand exit. "I'm going home for a few days. We can handle the lease when I return. You are set until the end of the quarter anyway, since you paid it in full already."

Sarah didn't move. Her face concealed in the pillow on the floor. I had only been out of the room an hour at the most, packing up my life for my departure. She remained motionless. I crept up beside her and placed my foot beneath her stomach area to nudge her a bit. "Sarah, get up, stop playing. It's not that serious. They have cures and medication for all that now. Back in the day, it was a plague; but now unfortunately it's common," I joked just in case she was still feeling uptight about everything disclosed earlier. She didn't respond, almost like she planned to ignore me when I came in the room.

"Sarah!" I became furious. *Who would play this type of game?* I had not known her to be a jokester, but I had not known her at all. We had recently met with the start of school and most of the time she had been away at work or with her boyfriend. I really didn't even know where she worked. She told me, of course, but through all the chaos, it slipped my mind.

I stooped down beside her to flip her over with my hands, since it was beyond a joking situation. It took everything in me to hurl her body over to her back. Her body weighed much more than I imagined upon first glance. A faint hue of grayish-blue veiled her face. She no longer possessed her normal coloration. I fell backward and gasped for air—for the both of us. Her face seemed bloated. She did not take a breath. My initial thought was she was dead. I noticed the half-empty bottle of Xanax pills wrapped in her fingers, then I knew she was dead. I wanted to run. In all the movies I watched, when you stayed at the scene, you could be a potential suspect in the murder.

"Sarah. Wake up! Sarah. No! Sarah, Sarah!"

The passenger next to me lightly tapped me on my shoulder and woke me from my sleep.

"Are you okay? You were having quite a nightmare there." The middle-aged, blonde-haired woman stroked my shoulder, hoping I didn't go into some type of shock. Her son was sound asleep across her lap in the middle seat between us. "Before we even took off, you were knocked out. You must have been really tired." She smiled, still awaiting the signal that I was OK.

I looked back at her and smiled; nodding to ensure her I would be all right. The cool air from the overhead vents sent a chill across my body. We were preparing for our final descent into Oakland. My ears popped with every drop in elevation. I couldn't help but wonder how much of my dream was fiction versus reality. My reality lay right before me, back in Oakland, right where I had recently left to get away from all the drama and the pain. My body remained slightly sore from the minor surgery, so all of my movements were gradual. Although uneasy about being back in Oakland, I was grateful to exit the stuffy plane.

"Are you visiting Oakland or returning home?" She didn't go away. I hoped I could just blink my eyes and she would disappear from next to me. I did not prepare to have a conversation with her. I knew as soon as I answered the first question that another one was sure to follow. Next thing you know, she would know my life story. I had no choice in the matter. She seemed like a concerned nurturing woman, hoping I was not a troubled Foster kid who had no future and needed her divine saving. Every time a White person took time out of their day to engage in a conversation with me, I thought it to be for two reasons: to do me some kind of harm or to save me.

"Just visiting." I replied, turning away from her so she would end the conversation. As instructed by the flight attendant, I pulled up my seat and secured the tray table for landing. We received notification from the captain that we were preparing to land.

"Who is Sarah?" she requested inquisitively, not taking notice of the signs that I truly did not want to engage in any further conversation.

"Sarah is my roommate." The plane jilted. I cringed in my seat, closing my eyes to prepare for the bumpy landing.

"Well, is she alright? You were calling for her in your sleep." I kept my eyes closed, hoping the nice, kind, nosy lady would die first upon impact. *I'm kidding.*

"Well, I can tell that you are troubled. I am a psychologist out of San Francisco." She slid me her card with all of her contact information. "Call me when you are ready to talk and don't worry about the cost." She winked at me like we had some sort of mutual bond. I didn't want to appear rude, so I thanked her for the invitation. I wouldn't dare burst her captain-save-a-ho bubble by informing her that Black people don't go to therapy. Just as the thought released from my mind, she continued, "I know African-Americans don't typically choose to go to therapy, but you may find it is just what you need to get beyond the hurt." With the ability to read my mind like that, I was already on the road to conversion.

I placed the card in my carry-on bag side-pocket for safe-keeping. The plane thudded against the runway and came to a screeching halt. Our bodies jerked forward and the little boy that once lay fast asleep jumped up with the movement of the

153

plane, wiping his eyes; holding onto his mother. She embraced him and rubbed his back, whispering in his ear, *everything will be OK. We are home now.*

# Chapter 15

Sweets Ballroom contained the usual afternoon crowd for a weekday. The majority of the patrons came on the weekend for events and happy hour specials. Charles went ahead and scheduled a meeting with the owner to discuss ways for him to pay restitution, considering the courts ordered him to do so. Despite the demands of the court to pay the fine, his business relationship with Rufus Brown, the newly appointed club manager, superseded their declaration, and his operation was set in motion. Charles' reputation with the ladies and patrons around town kept the place packed on several occasions, hosting parties throughout the year and offering security services when his business was in a slump.

"My Man, Chuck! How are you holding up?" Rufus shined his solid gold tooth with a smile, showing the distinction between his temporary grill and his permanent teeth. He slapped Charles on the back where he sat at the bar. Rufus was about twenty years older, and ten years behind on all the fashion trends. He was in his early fifties and holding on to the little style he could, but he reigned as a businessman. His silk gold-trimmed shirt and powder blue socks gave the impression that even when men rocked the style, he didn't quite have it.

"What's up Rufus? I'm glad you could work this out for me,"

his response not nearly as jovial as Rufus'.

"You know I got you, son. Plus, Edmond is a good man. He called me up and told me about everything." Rufus grabbed a bar stool beside him, climbed atop and told the bartender to whip him up his favorite drink, *Hennessey* straight.

"I got a lot going on right now," Charles started, taking a sip of his water. After two incidents occurring out of his control due to being drunk, he had more than learned his lesson. He thought it best to stop drinking for a while. "My boy was murdered." He placed his head down, clenching the glass in his hand.

"I heard." Rufus interrupted, placing a friendly hand on his shoulder to let him know he didn't have to continue explaining if he was not ready.

"I'll get you the money I owe you, just as soon as all of this is over." He lifted his head and quickly put his head back down in shame.

"Don't you worry about all of that; I told you I got you! The debt is damn near paid off already."

"How?" Charles perked up, raising his head in shock.

"Don't worry about it. Now I have some other business to handle. Take your time." He gave him two more friendly pats on the back and finished the remainder of his drink. He tipped the bartender and retreated back to his office.

A calm came over Charles after he left. All the frustration and worry began to subside, almost as if things for him were on the verge of turning around.

He decided that it came time for him to face his boy. Charles had gone AWOL. He needed time to sort everything out, and the thoughts and opinions of others just posed an imminent distraction for him. It came time to pick up his phone and speak to the public. Lance was first on the list to contact. He reluctantly dialed his number, knowing that as soon as Lance picked up, he would give him an earful. Oddly, Lance didn't give him a hard time. Charles informed Lance of his location at Sweets and his agreement with Rufus to work out the payment for the damages. Charles knew Lance would try his best to help him get the money if he had to pull from his own savings, but he had already done enough. All he requested was for him to meet him down there immediately.

"What's up, Bruh?" Lance walked directly to the bar and took the seat on the opposite side of Charles. Lance was concerned and relieved that he was alive and well. Without warning, he grabbed a hold of Charles, creating an awkward moment between the two of them and held him, breaking all guy codes. Charles welcomed the embrace. He couldn't front. He missed his boy. He sniffled, hoping to maintain his cool and hard-core facade.

"The funeral is Saturday morning. Mrs. Naples sent me the information yesterday and she would like us to participate. I told her we would be available to do whatever she needed." Charles quickly tried to loosen his words without breaking his character; but it was useless; he couldn't fight back the tears any longer. A droplet surfaced in his left eye, then his right. He didn't even attempt to wipe them away; the stream came flowing down. They briefly sat in the element of silence, paying respect for their fallen brother.

"If we need to take care of the dude who did this, I'm down!" Lance stated matter-of-factly, breaking the silence between them. Word traveled around town, as Darnise informed him, but he didn't know if Charles had gotten wind of any news. He had been off the grid for all he knew and out of the loop.

"Darnise told me that they were not after Elijah."

"Did you talk to the police?" Charles casually turned and set down his water, ignoring Lance's previous statement. He didn't raise his voice, just shifted his head to make eye contact with Lance. "The police came by my mama's salon asking questions and threatening to arrest me for the murder of Tony Watkins, Tanisha's brother. They didn't have any evidence, so they let me go. Did they come questioning you?"

"They brought me in for questioning. Same story. They didn't have any proof, so they let me go." Lance answered, holding back the information as to the entirety of the situation that transpired. He was hesitant. The course the conversation was on made him a bit uncertain of where Charles was headed.

"Calvin Rogers showed up at my mama's shop. I walked in on him talking to my mama." All of Charles' remarks seemed broken and scattered, as if he was attempting to put together a puzzle.

"What does Calvin got going wit yo' mama?" Lance asked, with total confusion beaming from his facial expression.

"Charlene tried to insinuate that he was my biological father, but I'm not accepting that! I don't care if he is, anyway. He ain't been in my life thus far, and he never will." Charles spoke in the rhythmic pattern as a drunken man, yet he was sober.

"Charlene Tucker was there too? How did all this come together? I gotta admit, Edmond is a pimp!" He reached out his fist to give Charles dap, but he looked back at him like his hand had a disease. Lance understood and pulled his fist back and dapped it himself. *I know he's a pimp* he mumbled under his breath.

"How are you holding up with all of this? Where have you been?" Lance questioned, changing the subject.

"Remember Shorty from the Shadow Bar?"

"The waitress?"

"Nah, the young, fine chick you left wit."

"Jamie-Lynn?"

"Yeah her. She let me crash at her place."

"What the hell do you mean?" Lance rose up from his seat, leaning in toward Charles to get in his face.

"Oh, so you mad? I'm joking. It doesn't feel good, does it? I crashed at the waitress' house for a couple days. She showed a brotha a lotta love. She played hard to get at first, but you know I don't play to lose," he smirked as he took another sip of his water.

"Well, I guess it worked out that I didn't take her number that night, huh?" Lance spat back at Charles, proving he had one-upped him. "You very well could have been with Jamie-Lynn." Lance stated, sitting back in his chair, feeling silly for confronting his friend about a situation he had been guilty of. "I had her drop me off at Darnise's crib in West Oakland."

"You did what? You let that fine ass woman slip through yo' fingers. What were you thinking? Darnise has never been worth it!" he responded with disgust, shaking his head at his friend's brainless decisions.

"I didn't trust her. I just met the girl. I wanted to be where I knew I could be held down. Nisey has been down wit me fo' years." Lance motioned to the bartender to get him a drink—anything. The bartender had been listening to the entirety of the conversation. He decided on a Heineken beer and popped the lid.

"That girl is trash! No offense, but the girl has been making yo' life a living hell since day one. I don't see how you deal wit' these ghetto broads." The bar tender shook his head at

159

Charles' statement, disappointed that a fellow brother fell for the okie-doke.

"I can't help myself. It is something about a chick with cornrows, piercings, and tats that just turns me on," he chuckled at his own crazy logic. "But you know, Darnise left me hanging this morning and all I could think about was Jamie-Lynn. I think I am going to go see her and make things right."

"Bruh, whatever you do, make sure you hit it one time for me." They clashed their glasses together in a toast and continued their "catch up" session.

Jamie-Lynn had just released the last of her kids to the final recess of the day. She was exhausted. The children had been extra rambunctious, high on the fruit snacks and graham crackers donated by a parent who worked at the local Target. She convinced the company to give to the school for being the top elementary school in the city for the quarter. Jamie sat comfortably at her desk, shuffling through paperwork that she constantly put off completing due to her lack of energy.

"Knock, knock," he said seductively. Lance stood head cocked with his sexy-eye-scowl, staring straight at her, as she remained seated at the desk, waiting for her to invite him in.

She tried her very best to ignore him and avoid eye contact, knowing his eyes had the ability to tug and pull her back in luring her into his aura. "What do you want?" she uttered, keeping her head down; pretending to be preoccupied by her paperwork.

"I came by to see you." He walked in, assuming that the invitation he was in search of would not be given. He strolled around behind her cluttered desk and stood directly behind where she sat, allowing his scent to penetrate her nostrils.

"What are you doing here? I am at work, and I don't have time for your games. You chose who you wanted that night and I received it loud and clear," she spoke firmly, not turning around to acknowledge his presence behind her, but the battle between her inner self and her mind was nearing defeat.

He stooped down, pulled back her hair, and kissed her on her neck. She jerked to the side and swatted at him like he was an annoying fly. "Don't be like that," he moaned. He pushed her paperwork aside, plopped down on her desk and leaned in to grab her chin to get her to focus on him. "I can't stop thinking about you," he gazed into her eyes, hoping that would do the trick.

"Lance, you don't get it," she protested, pushing his hand away from her chin and rose up to gain a better position for the interaction. "I was willing to take you as you were, no judgment..." she stopped mid-sentence and just shook her head. "I'm not going to do this here... I refuse."

"Ms. Johnson? Are you OK?" a pint-sized voiced echoed from the hallway as he wiped his eyes. To him, it looked like Ms. Johnson was in some sort of trouble.

"I'm fine, Mario. Thank you for checking on me. Go back outside with the other children until the bell rings."

"Don't worry Lil Man, I'll take care of her," Lance called back to him as the little boy turned and sprinted back outside to recess, convinced that her words were true.

"It is time for you to go. My kids will be back in here soon and I have to get ready for their science lab," she pushed out; frustrated that she had to go through this with him. In her mind, she had it all figured out. She would swoop in, save him from the unnecessary drama from the ghetto no-good women in his life. He would see the amazing woman in her; change his ways, wife her and they would live happily ever after. However, reality made things far more difficult.

"Before I go, just hear me out." Lance grabbed a hold of her wrist as she turned to walk away from him to retire to her desk. She allowed him to continue; her curiosity had total control of the situation. "There is something about you that I just can't deny. I know I messed up. I got scared. I wanted to be with somebody who I thought had my back, but all I could think about was you. I don't really know you and you may think you know me and have me figured out, but there is more. All I want is the opportunity to show you that in one night you had an effect on me. I can't say what it was, but I know I want to do everything in my power to see what we could be."

Jamie closed her eyes and took in a deep breath. "My father works for the police department as an investigator. I called him after I dropped you off to keep you protected."

"Protected from what?" he requested, letting go of her hand.

"When I went to see my father the other day; before we met, I saw this woman filing a report against you. I knew it was you from all the stories from your mom. She fit the description and so did you, so I decided to investigate." Lance looked at her with bewilderment as she continued. "Then it all made sense when I came down to The Shadow Bar and we ran into her outside, your girlfriend. She was at the station with Tanisha and they were plotting against you. When you had me drop you off at her house, I knew you didn't have a clue; so I called my daddy to take care of it."

"That bitch set me up? Is that what you are telling me?" he yelled in frustration that his boy had hit the nail on the head.

"Lance!" she harshly whispered back, reminding him he was at an elementary school and she would not tolerate his inappropriate language. The recess bell sounded and all the kids came rushing into the classroom, taking a seat at their assigned tables. "We can finish this later."

"Oh, so I can see you again?" Lance perked up a bit, licking his lips and smoothing his goatee with confidence.

"I guess…" she lowered her eyes, but smiled inside. She really couldn't resist him and she had every intention of allowing him back in if he came and requested it.

"Oooo Ms. Johnson has a boyfriend," one of the little girls sang out to the awaiting class, causing all the children to giggle, making Ms. Johnson feel appreciated and embarrassed all at the same time.

"How about this? Give me a call when you get off and we can meet up somewhere to finish this conversation." He gently kissed her on her hand. "Kids, make sure you take care of my girlfriend while I am gone." He winked at her out of the corner of his eye and walked out as all the kids laughed and giggled at their teacher.

# Chapter 16

As soon as the confession left Samson's lips, Edmond was livid. The fact that Calvin Rogers had gotten to his son disturbed his spirit. He fought hard to keep Calvin from destroying Charles's life and right under his nose, Calvin was trying to tear his family apart. Calvin had love for Raquel—this is true—but he didn't possess the unconditional love that ignited the fuse in a man to do whatever it takes to keep his family safe. He only knew money. It was his only motivation. If Edmond was to get through to Calvin and ultimately get even to free Samson from his binding contract, he had to meet him on his level.

"Did you tell anyone that you killed him?" Edmond paced back and forth scratching his head, uneasy about how Samson got mixed up with all this madness. "This is all my fault! I shouldn't have let you out of my sight," still pacing and shaking his head in disbelief. "Who am I foolin'? You would have done this, anyway." He remarked to no one in particular, still pacing. *Where did he get a gun? Who sold it to him?* He couldn't fathom how his son was able to get his hands on a real gun. Samson always spoke a good game and for him to back it up; in a strange and unusual way, made Edmond proud. He spent many years trying to get Samson to be about his business. This was not the road he envisioned, but it illustrated to him that his many lectures didn't fall on deaf ears.

There was no way he would allow his son to go to prison. He had to devise a plan to ensure that his son would not go down for murder. Samson may have thought it was cool to be a thug until he would be forced to spend quality time with the real ones in prison. Oakland had enough young boys being killed daily or hauled off to jail. There was no eminent need for Samson to be a victim as well. It was his daily mission to keep his son from being a statistic. Samson was twenty years old and already blessed to have made it past his eighteenth birthday.

The day before Samson's eighteenth birthday, he caught AC Transit with a few of his boys to the East Oakland Youth Development Center on 82nd and International for a pickup game of basketball. On his way back from the local liquor store, a slightly older young man, who didn't recognize him as being favorable in his neighborhood, held him up at gunpoint. His saving grace came when a cop car rolled past and the boy took off running. Samson made up in his mind that if he was going to earn respect in the streets, he had to be strapped. It was the only language the young men understood. Those who have, take from those who don't. Simple.

Samson hesitated before responding, recalling his actions, "I... I told the chick I was staying with, but I didn't give her any names."

"You did what? You are more stupid than I thought." Edmond scolded. He tried his best to refrain from putting his hands on him again. Physical abuse would not assist in the situation, considering it led to the initial reason for his leaving. "I know I taught you better than to run yo' mouth in the streets."

"I only told her!" Samson remarked, hoping to get some slack for keeping the numbers down to only one. He shifted in his seat and braced himself for his father's response. He evaded the question about the gun because he promised Elijah that he would keep it between them.

"Don't you know telling a woman anything is telling the streets? Women talk. They talk to each other, they talk to their family and they talk to their man! Hell, you hear yo' mama and sister gossiping all the time about other people's business?" He continued to pace. "You sure you didn't tell any of yo' little patnas? You know how y'all youngsters like to brag."

"Nah... I couldn't get a hold of 'em."

"Samson, I need you to realize that there is no viable reason for you to be in these streets. Did we not do our job as parents for you growing up?"

"Pops, that's not it!"

"Well... what is it, son?" He questioned with frustration, throwing his hands up to the sky. "Tell me!"

"I don't know. I don't have an answer for you."

"Do you think we don't love you and you had to go out in the streets looking for love?"

"Nah... You are turning this into something it is not."

"Maybe you just don't understand what all this means." Charlene remained silent to allow the father son exchange to happen. It was well overdue. It was rare that the two of them had a conversation devoid of raised voices. "I worked hard, so my children...scratch that, so my son would not have to worry about running the streets or taking another man's life, and for what? Money?"

The guilt of Samson's actions began to settle in and rest on heavy his shoulders. The impact of his actions on his family never crossed his mind. He thought he was retaliating against his father for threatening him with leaving the house. In his mind, he was teaching his father a lesson for allowing him to walk out of the protection of his care.

"I did it for the money and to prove to you that I am a man and I can get it on my own!"

"Okay. Okay. I think I have a plan. Call up Mr. Calvin Rogers and let him know you are ready to put in some work tonight. Tell him to pick you up from the house. I will work out the rest." Edmond exited the room to the back house to enact the initial steps of his master plan. He didn't want Samson to know what he was up to, because he was sure to blow the plan if he knew too many of the details. It was best for him not to know. Unfortunately, all this called for Edmond to retreat back to his former ways, but if it meant keeping his family safe, he was willing to go the distance.

He gently closed the door to the man cave and pulled out his cellular device. He knew the number by heart and didn't bother scrolling through his contacts.

"Hey Rocky, it's me Ed. I need you to do me a favor. It's time that I cash in that *'I'll do whatever you need me to do,'* for all the times I had your back." She agreed, as he knew she would. He hung up the phone, convinced that his plan would put an end to all the drama once and for all.

Samson waited on the porch dressed in an all-black hoodie and his dark wash 501 Levi's jeans and black gloves as Calvin requested. It was a quarter past nine. The sun had fully set, and the onset of the darkish blue night hue overtook the sky. He flopped down on the side of the porch, rubbing his hands

167

together to keep them warm, waiting for the black Cadillac to pull up. He hated knowing that he willingly put his family in jeopardy.

Out of the corner of his eyes, he noticed a black Lexus pull up and park in front of the neighbor's house. The driver turned off the engine, but didn't get out. From where Samson was seated on the porch, it was difficult to make out the identity of the driver. After five minutes or so of waiting and watching, he shrugged it off as someone who may be lost in the neighborhood. The Tuckers lived in a decent neighborhood where poverty and violence were almost non-existent. It was relatively normal to get outside visitors. Just as Samson contemplated backing down from the plan, the awaited vehicle pulled up in front of the house. The window lowered, and a hand motioned for him to get into the car. He hustled over to the opposite side and let himself in. In his short time working for Calvin, he learned quickly not to keep him waiting.

"What's up Young Blood? So you think you are ready to put in the real work now?" Calvin snickered at the thought of Samson feeling as though he was a man now. "You remind me a lot of myself when I was your age, always eager to get your hands dirty!" Calvin Rogers consistently stayed suited up, ready for business. His tailored gray suit sparkled. It wasn't flashy, but it was clear it was expensive and he didn't buy it out of a department store.

Calvin's phone chirped, taking his attention away from Samson for a brief moment to handle the incoming call. He cleared his throat and slightly lowered his voice. "Rocky, what do you want? I'm trying to take care of some business. I don't have time to go back and forth with you."

"I need you to come down to the shop. There are some men

here that I think you may want to speak with. And they have guns." Raquel responded through the phone, unfazed by his unwelcoming greeting. She didn't appear frightened, but he knew her to handle her own and mask her fear when she was truly afraid.

"Why didn't you call your son *Rambo?* I think he is quite capable of taking care of this situation for you. Plus, I am not going to take too many more threats from him if he decides to show up again."

"I can't reach him! Please come and help me. Plus, they requested you specifically. They mentioned that you have something that is extremely valuable to them and are willing to pay you a hefty amount to retrieve it." Raquel cried out, exposing her shielded emotions and desperation. She hoped it would be enough for him to come to her rescue.

"Dammit! How much money are we talking? Forget it... I'm on my way." He hung up the phone and turned to Samson. "I guess we are going to take a quick detour, Young Blood."

The block in which the salon was located lay barren—no cars or people in-sight. The businesses in the community were closed for the evening not to return until sunrise. He instructed his driver to pull around to the back of the lot. Piedmont was known for being a quiet, predominantly White neighborhood. Any Black men with guns would immediately alarm the neighbors and the police would be present in five seconds flat.

It seemed slightly too suspicious for Calvin to go in and assess the situation; his years of dealing in the streets, and with Raquel, taught him a great deal about being cautious. He tapped Samson on his shoulder and slid him the Glock 9mm pistol. "I want you to go inside and shoot anything moving.

169

Do you understand Young Blood? Anything." Calvin nodded his head for reassurance and to let him know he was free to go handle the task. Piedmont Police Department did not fancy Calvin, yet he had a few of them on his payroll as well.

"Are you sure about this, Calvin? It doesn't look like anyone is here," he eased out. He didn't want his apprehension to show. Calvin turned his head away, communicating to him it was time to get out of the car and take care of business.

Samson slowly navigated his way out of the car, contemplating what his father had got him wrapped up in. The lot had no sign of light from light posts or buildings nearby. He crept closer to the back entrance, clenching the pistol in the palm of his hand. He whispered the Lord's Prayer with each step he took. Although he had made it through the first portion of the initiation process, he was not prepared for what lay behind the doors, possibly lurking in the dark corners of the salon. It could be an ambush attack. For all he knew, Calvin could have set it all up for him to get killed.

He noticed the same car that was parked outside of his parents' house must have been trailing them because it was parked in the lot of the salon. Everything about the scenario did not sit right with Samson. He thought back on all the times he wished for this type of lifestyle or bragged about living it; but at this very moment, he wanted out. The idea of being killed or somehow endangering his family removed all desire of the thug life. It seemed like the likely road to take for his peers. It was saturated in the culture, the music, and society. Even with his knowledge that his father had lived the same life. It was like it was a set-up from day one for him to get involved in drugs and violence. Unsure of what lay behind the walls of the salon provided him his moment of clarity, but he refused to turn back. It was his decision to get involved in this predicament, and he was going to see it through. Samson griped the gun in his hand and raised it up in front of his face about a few inches from his nose for the best aim. As he stepped closer, the sound of rustling in the salon made his heart beat faster.

"Calvin! I am so glad you are here." Raquel rushed to his passenger side door. "Why are you sitting in the car?"

"I sent the Young Blood in to check everything out."

"What? What do you mean?"

"You know Edmond's boy, Samson? I sent him in to take care of the situation. That is what you wanted, right?"

"Why is he working for you?" she demanded.

"He wanted to make some money. It was the least I could do."

"You sent a little boy in to handle it? Are you crazy? He could get hurt or killed?" The panic in her tone became more apparent.

"Maybe that's the plan. Are you worried about the seed of the man that left you to take care of another woman? You keep making these bad choices, Baby Doll," he slid his hand out the window in an attempt to caress her face that she immediately blocked.

"That may be so, but I am glad that I didn't have to put up with you."

"But yet you called me here to take care of you. Now where are these men that have requested my presence?"

"I requested your presence." Calvin recognized the familiar voice.

"Edmond Tucker, I've been waiting for you to pop up and show your face." Calvin smiled. Intimidation was far from an emotion Calvin experienced.

"Well, here I am. And I believe you have something that is extremely valuable to me. You see, I understand my son has been working for you... that ends tonight."

"Well, Edmond, you know how business works. We must be talking money." Calvin opened the passenger door and stepped out to speak face-to-face. He motioned to the driver to keep his seat with the engine running.

"We can talk money. How much to leave my son alone and get back to your business as usual?" Edmond moved in closer. The space between the men grew cold. The hostility from years of enmity lingered in the air.

"I don't want to run your little pockets for too much, so let's say $100,000. This keeps you, your son and my mouth shut when the Feds come looking for who murdered Tony Watkins."

*Pow! Pow! POW!* The shots rang out in the night air. *Silence.* Everything lay still. No movement. This time, he didn't tremble or shake. His nerves were surprisingly calm. Everyone stood in shock as the blood rolled down his face from the micro-sized hole in his forehead.

Finally, Raquel gasped in terror at what she had just witnessed. Edmond turned to his son, that had his gaze affixed on Calvin's lifeless body.

"Is he dead?" He refused to lower the gun until his death was confirmed.

"He is dead, son?" Edmond steadily made his way toward his son. It was no need to check. Samson had precise aim.

"Good. Now, what exactly was *your* plan?"

Raquel did not know what to make of the scene. He had been a thorn in the flesh for so many people, yet her love for him remained.

Samson decided after he didn't find a soul lurking in the salon that he would come back out to the vehicle. When he saw his father and Raquel and no one else in sight besides the driver, he thought it best to just follow the directions given and shoot what he saw moving. Not to mention, Calvin had given him his gun. It would look like suicide or worse, a set-up. Either way, his prints were not on it and were no longer a concern for his family. Samson shifted the gun in the direction of the driver.

"We can make this a double homicide. Just say the word." Samson was in full control of the situation. The beast in him emerged as he locked eyes with the dedicated chauffeur. The driver fiercely shook his head and placed his arms high-up in the air, surrendering. "I suggest you get out of here before the police think you did this. Think about it. The driver will be the ultimate suspect." He hurried out of the car and ran into the night to flee from the scene.

# Chapter 17

"Mama, I'm coming thru." Lance hung up, closed the phone, and tossed it in the passenger seat. He was so elated that Jamie Lynn actually kept her word and called him up after she got off work. They worked out a few of the kinks of their relationship, and she agreed to have a nice, intimate dinner with Lance and his mom. It would be more of a shock than surprise for Lydia, because she had not been aware of their relationship woes. She was oblivious to it all.

He pulled up to her single-family home located right outside of North Oakland in Berkeley, bumping Usher "Confessions." He hopped out, opened the door for Jamie, and they both made their way up to the porch.

"Is that my handsome baby coming through to see his mama?" Lydia barely waited for him to make it through the door before she started laying kisses all over his face. "Oh, and he brought my favorite girl with him too! Come here, girl, and give Mama some sugar too."

"Hi Miss Lydia. As you can see, I did what you told me to do." Jamie stated matter-of-factly and blushed.

"I am so happy for you two. So, tell me all about it. When is the wedding?" She squeezed Jamie's cheek like she was a six-year-old little girl.

"Wow. Mama, slow down. We just met. Give me some time to get to know the girl." Lance reminded.

"Boy, you don't have time! This woman is the total package. You better wife her up before the next man does." She turned and winked at Jamie, then gave her a nudge to back her up and let him know she was a hot commodity. Jamie Lynn cleared her throat to remind the two of them that she was still present in the room, feeling slightly embarrassed.

"Well, I made dinner, so you two just come on in the kitchen and fix your plates so we can catch up." She made her way back to the kitchen to prepare the table to eat. She put together a grand spread as only Miss Lydia could pull off. Jamie grabbed plates, forks and knives to assist in setting the table, as she often did with her grandmother when it was time for dinner. "I ran into Raquel the other day at the Marriott and it looked as though she was still creeping around. It's no wonder why Charles is reckless!"

"Mama!" Lance shouted. "You have no right to judge." Miss Lydia could not resist sharing her gossip with her lack of friends; she spilled most of the tea to Lance.

"I may not have a right to judge, but that woman has slept with all the officials in Oakland. I know how Charles got out of that jail time, but I'm going to mind my business because I know that is yo' friend and we have company. By the way...how is he doing?"

"He's hanging in there. I met up with him at The Shadow Bar. He is laying low for a while."

"The Shadow Bar? I heard about that boy Elijah on the news that was murdered there. They said he had been involved in some kind of gang war. I don't want you going around that place anymore."

"That's a lie!" Lance slammed his fist down on the counter in the kitchen where he stood, startling them both with his outrage. "Mama, you know that was my boy."

"Then he must have been doing something illegal if somebody wanted him dead. I tried to tell you about hanging around them thugs."

"Mama, we are not going to have this conversation right now. I don't want to be disrespectful to you or your home, so please drop it!" She sensed that it was too soon to pry and dig deep into the situation. She glanced over to Jamie for confirmation, but she remained silent with her head facing down. As a mother, it was her duty to be concerned, but not at the expense of someone else; she opted to digress.

"OK, baby, I'll let it go. I just don't want to see anything like that happen to you." Lance allowed the moment to pass to keep from getting worked up all over again. He was grateful, in a better place mentally; especially since Jamie decided to give him another chance. He promised himself to make every attempt to keep it right.

Just as they were seated ready to bless the food; like clockwork, there was a loud banging against the door.

"Mama, are you expecting someone?" Lance blurted out in frustration, tossing his utensils down on the table.

"Now you know that you are the only person who stops by here." Lydia sat still in her seat. She was convinced that the knocking guest was not for her. "Unless you have a surprise date for me?"

"Lance, open up! We need to talk."

"Boy, you need to get a handle on these little girls. I can't keep having them stopping by my house, causing trouble." Lydia pulled her plate in closer to her and indulged. She refused to allow one of Lance's girl-toys to disturb yet another meal. "I'm going to eat and you need to get the door."

"I don't even know who that is, Mama." He refused to even look in Jamie's direction. He knew that this was not the way to get back into her good graces.

Jamie quickly hopped up, dodging his attempt to grab her, and ran over to the door. She was so amped up about the stranger behind the door; she didn't take the time to check to see who it was. Lance and his mother were so comfortable discussing personal matters in her presence, she felt right at home. Secretly, she was hoping it was Darnise to confront her face-to-face.

"What do you want?" Jamie demanded to the knocking guest.

"I want to speak with Lance. I don't want any trouble with you; I'm here to set things straight with him." The young lady looked Jamie up and down, holding her belly and composure.

"Lance, your baby mama is at the door. I think you may want to handle this one on your own." She rolled her eyes clear to the back of her skull and released the door to Lance.

He took in a deep breath and gathered himself up from the table to face her. It had been a never-ending cycle, and things were well out of his control. Why should they stop now? He pondered to himself. He moved Jamie to the side and whispered for her to go back to the kitchen, so he could handle it. He gently kissed her cheek to show Tanisha that he had moved on and if she came to try to get him back in any way, she didn't have a chance. It didn't hurt to get some cool points with Jamie, either.

"So, what's up?" Lance leaned up against the edge of the door, propping up his back and folded his arms.

"A lot has happened since I was here last. I found out that the baby is not yours. I actually don't know who the father is." A sign of relief crossed Lance's face, allowing him to breathe easy. The weight of despair lifted from his shoulders and he actually listened to the remainder of what she had to say. "I didn't mean for my brother to get involved, but I had no other choice but to tell him you raped me. You put your hands on me and I was upset." Her voice went up a few octaves and tears welled in her eyes. "Because of this mess, I lost my brother, my only brother. I know you had nothing to do with it, but I just wanted to come to you and let you know that I am sorry." She shielded her face in shame, sobbing uncontrollably. Lance only watched, unsure of how to react. He wanted to console her, but that could easily send the wrong message. He didn't want to just shut the door on her, because believe it or not, he cared about her feelings. "Darnise came to me and convinced me that I should file charges against you to teach you a lesson. I feel terrible about everything and I just want to right my wrongs before I give birth to my child. I hope you can forgive me." She gradually turned and walked away without waiting for his response.

"Tanisha!" Lance called after her. She paused and turned to hear him. "It's all good. Take care of yourself. Let me know if you need anything. I know what you are going through, and I wouldn't wish that feeling on anyone."

He gently closed the door. Surprisingly, it was a hard pill for him to swallow. He considered the idea of being a father. It was not in his best interest to have a baby by a woman he didn't love, but his mother was right. If it was, in fact, his child, he would have stepped up to do his part.

"Baby, let's just thank God that it is not your child and that when the time is right, you will build your family." Lydia pressed her hand against his back, turned and winked at Jamie Lynn. "I just heard a mouthful. You have a lot of explaining to do! Now I don't want to have to go after Darnise and put hands on her, but I will, and I don't mean holy hands. You know Mama will do that."

"How about you call her up and have her to come over here? I think I want to share some words with her, loving, kind words." Jamie suggested, standing with her hand on her hip, motivated by his mother's intentions. "Call her up." She pointed to the cell on his hip.

Lance was reluctant to dial that number because he only imagined how it could all end. However, the idea of his new woman checking his ex was every man's fantasy. He proceeded to call her up. She answered and agreed to come over and talk.

As soon as Darnise pulled up, she shouted out the window for Jamie to come outside and face her like a woman. Jamie tried her best to keep her composure, but she did bring it upon herself. In her mind, she would come over, they would sit down like ladies and explain how Lance has moved on, and her services would no longer be needed in their lives. Yet, the devil had full control over her, and she couldn't resist him.

Jamie Lynn darted out of the house toward her vehicle. She flung open her door and yanked Darnise out by her freshly braided box-braids, unbothered by her oversize cousin, who sat next to her in the passenger seat. Darnise attempted to swing back in her direction and block her from getting a good grip, but she was ill prepared for the ambush. With all her might, Jamie maneuvered her body out of the car and dragged her into the grass of Miss Lydia's front yard. Jamie didn't really have a plan of attack and didn't intend to fight the girl, but her rage was unpredictable. She kicked and punched, missing more than she landed, as Darnise blocked her every attempt. "Get this ho' off of me," she screamed.

Her cousin scrambled around from the passenger side to the opposite side of the car to grab Jamie off of her. She locked her thick arm around her neck from behind and pulled her body weight down to free Darnise from her grip.

Lance allowed a few more landed blows before deciding to intervene. He needed to see how well Jamie could hold her own. The neighbors heard the squeals and yelling from the three women tussling outside of their homes and positioned themselves on the porch for a front-row seat to the action. The community was very familiar with Darnise and her drama. Many of them awaited the day that Lance would put on his big boy pants and let her go. For that reason, they delighted in the sudden showdown and thought it best to let them fight without the confusion and interference of law enforcement as long as it remained a bloodless battle.

"Okay, Okay, Okay. That's enough." Lance, who kept his distance on the steps, finally pulled Jamie from atop of her, advising her to get into the house. Darnise's cousin proved to be of little help. After her chokehold move, her air passage closed on her and she was left, wheezing off to the side of the yard, fighting for her next breath.

Lance glanced over Jamie's body, amazed at how she kept herself together. Her clothes were a bit tattered from the tussle however, she didn't have a scratch on her. Lance smiled inside. He was thoroughly impressed with her fighting skills. Shockingly, the sweet soul before him had hands. The feisty demeanor he witnessed before was out. He was clear of the reason he had been so attracted to her.

"So, this is what we do now? You set me up?" She slowly unwrapped herself from the fetal position. She placed her hands down as an anchor to regain her normal breathing pattern, wiping off sweat and a little blood from her lip resulting from her initial impact with the ground. She searched around for her partner in crime, who sat on the edge of the lawn gasping for air. She dusted the dirt from her jeans and blouse and continued her rant, "You get stank hoes to do your dirty work?"

"You got it all wrong, Baby. You set yourself up when you tried to get me locked up. I was down for you and I thought you had my back." Lance kept his distance, in case the rest of the "Zoo Crew" was standing by, waiting to attack. All she had to do was give the birdcall and they would come running. He did not desire to put his hands on her, or he might injure her for real.

"Lance, I had your back, even when you had every chick in the city in and out of your bedroom. So yes, you are damn right. I set you up. I couldn't kill yo' ass, so I tried the next best thing."

"Hold up! Are you trying to say you tried to get me killed? I know you are not saying that."

"Hell no, I'm not saying that. I just wanted to scare you a bit, but it went further than expected," she turned her face away to avoid the eye contact. "I told Tony to do what he had to do, but not to kill you. I didn't know you would leave the club and I didn't know that both you and Charles messed with Tanisha. Apparently, he got the two of you mixed up."

Lance charged at her and grabbed her by her neck. "Because of you, my boy is dead, and you got another man killed. You don't deserve to live. You think this is a game?" She wriggled in his grasp, choking for air. He tightened his grip with each phrase becoming more and more enraged.

"Lance, let her go right now!" Miss Lydia was furious. She watched from the window in the living room and could not take it any longer. She busted through the door to keep him from killing the girl, already ready with her hair pinned back to stay out of her face. She pried his fingers from the lock he had around her neck. Lance dropped her immediately as he came to from his brief blackout. "I will take care of this. Go in the house!"

Miss Lydia wanted to go to work on her like she was sixteen again fighting in the streets, but she knew Darnise was a troubled girl. She needed help more than anything and she had been battered enough. She whispered a quick word of prayer over her and let her lay in her quandary.

Jamie Lynn instantly got on the line and called up her father. She explained the situation to him. Five cop cars surrounded the house and instructed Ms. Brown to back away from the girl. The neighbors were already on standby to share their version of the story of how Jamie Lynn was attacked by the jealous ex-girlfriend, who was mad that her long-time boyfriend had moved on. The officers under the direction of Detective Johnson arrested Darnise and took her down to the station for booking.

# Chapter 18

Everything in the house looked just as it did when I left, cluttered. I hoped that with me being out of the house, they would attempt to clean up the place and have a garage sale of some sort. It was merely my high hopes. I had been eager to see Samson for a change; being away from him made me miss him a small bit. I guess being away does make the heart grow fonder. Growing up, we spent many summers together swimming and going to the park, when life was simple. Before jealously and animosity entered the picture. Before our eyes became wide, open to the ways of the world. Speaking on the phone just wasn't the same, and I needed to get the inside scoop on all the drama I had missed being away and why it was necessary for me to come all the way home.

"Debra, get your bags from out of the hallway." Charlene's nagging voiced roared in my ear. I nearly just arrived home and my mother already had a reason to complain. I reluctantly picked up my belongings to appease her and keep the peace. I took them to my former bedroom, now a converted office, to keep her off my back.

"Where are Dad and Samson?" I asked, hoping they were just working on something out in the backyard. The way my mother made it seem, my dad couldn't wait to see me and honestly, I was unsure if Samson had been welcomed back into the house. There was no physical sign. It was all my way of getting the scoop without dishing it out. Then it dawned on me that he didn't know I had sex, let alone been with a boy under his nose before I left; but with the news of the miscarriage, the cat was out of the bag. He probably wanted to send for me to strangle the life from my promiscuous body. Suddenly, my desire to know his whereabouts faded, and I quickly dropped the subject.

The vibration from my cell startled me.

*Did you make it? Sarah XOXO*

Seeing her text gave me a great sigh of relief that she was alive. Nightmares were the very reason I stayed away from watching scary movies. Any scary movie that played with the idea of demons sent my subconscious into high gear. I responded so she wouldn't freak out on me and quickly turned it off to keep her from bothering me for the duration of the trip. I liked the girl, but at times she could be a nuisance; talking of her and Brad wanting to be married due to an STD gave me a headache, whether it had been real or imagined.

The fatigue from the flight began to settle in. I decided to lie down for a moment to allow my body some much-needed rest since the woman on the plane was determined to keep me awake. Her persistence seemed genuine, but unwarranted. I closed my eyes and thought of all the possibilities of why I had been summoned back home. *Maybe Samson got a girl pregnant and my mother wanted everyone to know at the same time. Maybe my dad was finally going to retire, and we needed to make plans on what the next steps would be. Maybe my parents were going to get a divorce... God forbid that happen.* My eyes shot open. That thought didn't sit well with me, and I knew if I continued to let my mind wander, the thoughts would become more morbid and intense.

The light tap on the door reminded me that I was not in my dorm room alone to my wandering thoughts. I shifted my body to my side to receive the knocking guest.

"Debra, after you settle in; I need you to meet me in the kitchen." My mama sounded sweet for a change. It was awkward and strange, but I could get used to it. With a small amount of mustered-up strength, I raised my body from its former resting position.

I pulled out my complete U.C.R. Freshmen outfit, consisting of a t-shirt, hoodie, and sweatpants. I removed my traveling clothes, took a quick five-minute shower, and changed into my college girl attire. The weather in Oakland was always cooler than Southern California, so I always packed accordingly; plus, I really wanted to put some miles into my new outfit.

I did just as instructed and met my mom in the kitchen. She was prepping for dinner. I couldn't help but notice her shaking as she chopped the onions and bell peppers for the meal. Charlene was a strong woman, loyal to her man, quick to run at his every command, but still strong. I didn't often see her sweat. Yet she appeared bothered—troubled, almost.

"Mama, what's going on?"

"Nothing, Debra. Pass me the potatoes out of the pantry." She continued chopping, hoping I would drop it and move on.

"Why are you bleeding?" A thin layer of blood trickled down her hand as she chopped. She was so distracted by convincing me she was all right that she didn't even notice. She looked down at her hand and let out a small gasp. She hurried over to the sink, rinsed it off, and blotted it with a paper towel.

"Do you remember our conversation in the hospital?" she

questioned, applying pressure to her wound.

"Yes. I do." I remembered that heart-to-heart like it was yesterday.

"The woman that I told you, your father dated in high school and beyond; well we had a minor altercation. She tried to attack me and I shoved her to the floor."

"You were fighting, Mama?" I couldn't believe what I was hearing. *Why were they even in the same location?* Her story didn't add up to me. "What? How? When?" My stuttering made my confusion more obvious.

"It was your father's bright idea for me to go to her salon for her to do my hair for our anniversary."

I was so anxious to get answers, I just cut her off midway through her explanation. "So you mean to tell me, *my* father advised *you* to go down to the salon and get your hair done by the other woman? In what world is that a good idea? Even I know that was a dumb decision." The story was extremely outrageous. I had to speak to her as if she were my roommate, Sarah.

"In the world where a wife does as her husband instructs." My father bullied his way into the conversation as he often did their relationship. He entered the kitchen, went straight for the refrigerator, and popped the cap of his last Heineken. I wanted to jump up and run into his arms, but I opted not to give my father my attention. I honestly didn't know if it was safe yet. I would officially greet him when she finished, and the air was clear. My mom simply ignored his presence and continued.

"The woman, Raquel, has a son named Charles—the one I told you about. I walked in on Raquel having a conversation with Calvin Rogers and I insinuated to Charles that he was his biological father. Well, Rocky didn't like that and attacked me." She placed the pile of chopped potatoes in a large bowl filled with cold water to keep preserved while she finished chopping the additional veggies for the stew.

"You had no business saying anything to that woman. We had an agreement." Edmond hissed at her as he walked over and gave me a kiss on my forehead with his wet beer lips. I wiped the residue from my face.

"You had no business sleeping with her either, but that didn't stop you now, did it?" I somehow no longer felt comfortable in the room. They had so much healing to do. I was relieved when Samson walked through the door to join the commotion in the kitchen.

"Samson! You're home." I popped up and raced over to embrace him. Initially, it felt awkward, but I quickly got over myself and savored the moment.

"Ewww. Get off of me!"

"You know you like it!" He tried his best to act like he didn't want my love, but I knew the truth. "Where are you two coming from?"

"We were out. That's all yo' big head needs to know!"

"Whatever!" I rolled my eyes at him. "What was so important that I had to come all the way out here?"

"I just wanted to see my family together again to celebrate this wondrous occasion." My father poked out his chest with a huge grin on his face. Charlene quickly cut her eyes over to Edmond, looking for an explanation. She knew that was not the reason for them calling her back home.

"What occasion?" I asked in confusion.

I watched as my father approached my mother and got down on one knee. She grabbed her chest and began to pant. He pulled out a beautiful, double-French-set halo diamond band platinum engagement ring. As a tear rolled down his face, I witnessed history in the making.

"Charlene Tucker, my wife, my lover, my best friend; I love you with all that is in me. You are the only woman for me. I want to spend every day for the rest of my life making you happy. Will you make me the happiest man in the world and marry me? And this time, I will give you the wedding you deserve." He glared into her eyes, awaiting her response.

She turned to us to get our reaction. We nodded profusely at our endorsement of her decision. She turned back to Edmond and exhaled. She wiped the tears from her eyes and closed them for a moment. She thought about all they had endured over the years and the recent events. She opened her eyes and smiled. "YES!"

Edmond jumped up and embraced her in his arms. Samson pulled out the twelve long-stem roses he hid just outside of the kitchen and presented them to our mother. She was so overjoyed. She had waited all her life for this moment. I finally understood their relationship and her patience. She would have waited a lifetime for him to come around; unfortunately, it had to come through an abundance of pain and despair.

"Everything is taken care of," he whispered to her as he held her in his arms.

Although everything didn't go as planned, it ultimately was the plan. And I was elated that they called me all this way to experience it.

My father released my mother and came toward me with one additional red long-stem rose. Again, he lowered himself down on one knee, grabbed my hand and placed it between his. "Debra, I love you. You are my baby girl. I know how you may feel about the miscarriage and I am here for you." I immediately wrapped my arms around my daddy, letting him know he didn't need to say another word. He tenderly kissed my forehead and just held me in his arms. Who was I to think he would be so cruel? My daddy loved me and I knew it all along.

# Chapter 19

The ambiance of the church was filled with distress and worry felt by those present to witness the home-going celebration of Elijah Edward Naples. The oversize oak wood church doors welcomed all the parishioners to remember his life and legacy. There rested a lack of certainty in the matter regarding the motive for his murder, the altercation or his assailant; yet all surrendered their inquisition to pay respect for him and the family.

The church was nestled between 85th Avenue and E Street. Although, based in a rough neighborhood, it was founded upon the vision of maintaining a facility for the local congregation, as well as, the surrounding community, to have a comfortable place to worship. Elijah, who in the latter half of his life, had taken a leave of absence from the church to figure out life on his own; still kept his membership and every so often gave money toward the ministry. He was raised in the church and knew the Lord as his personal Savior. However, in his opinion, the years of feeling the tedium and demands of the Christian life, he distanced himself from what he knew to be his saving grace.

Growing up, his mother would not allow a Sunday to pass without attending. He sang in the children's choir and assisted with the usher board whenever needed. The moment his mother felt he had reached the age of understanding, she backed off of him to give him the opportunity to serve the Lord freely. His dedication didn't match hers; but he attended as often as he felt necessary. He believed that as long as he was good to people, he would receive the same in return.

The service was set to begin promptly at 11:00am. His family and friends sullenly made their way into the winsome sanctuary, unaccepting of the reality that lay before them. The stillness was piercing. Flowers, bouquets and floral arrangements plastered the floors, walls and casket. The choir, draped in their Sunday morning choir ensemble, silently soothed the spirits of the people with melodies from heaven. Elijah's mother thought it best to have a closed casket funeral. The beauty of the boy she remembered, as her only son, was stripped away by the bullets that penetrated his head and body, leaving him unrecognizable.

Raquel Simmons, Lydia Brown, Jamie Lynn Johnson, The Tucker family and others filed in the church quickly locating open seats prior to the commencement of the service. People came from near and far; the need for the use of the overflow balcony area told the story of the lives that he had touched in his time on earth. *C.P. Bannon Mortuary* took much of the burden off of Mrs. Naples, who had to endure the entire process with only the assistance of her two daughters, since her late husband was overtaken by drug overdose when Elijah was a small boy. Times were often difficult, taking on the responsibility of being the sole provider and steward of her children. She sacrificed her own life and desires, hoping that her children had the best and did not go without. It was the reason Elijah hustled so hard. He hated to see his mother in pain. Her stress became his stress; therefore, he stepped up whenever required.

Lance and Charles adorned in their all-black suits and dark *Ray Ban* sunshades served as pallbearers for the service, along with a few of Elijah's cousins and childhood friends. They positioned themselves around the casket, offering up silent prayers for their brother. The two, still uneasy about the entire unfolding of events, agreed to put the search and seizure of the one responsible for his murder behind them. The word on the street conveyed that the infamous Calvin Rogers had exterminated his killer, anyway. Lance never mentioned to Charles about Darnise's semi-confession, because she was in jail. He figured that one day they would have that talk over plenty of liquor.

The service was short and sweet. The preacher who eulogized Elijah spoke immensely on forgiveness and transformation. His words pricked every heart in the building. Charles couldn't help but to feel the conviction of how he treated his own father. When he heard the news that he had been murdered, he had no emotion, no connection. However, he made a promise to himself to be like Edmond and be there for his own when that day came around.

No different, Lance felt the conviction as well and finally turned his life over to Christ. He knew the error of his ways for a long time and the angel in the form of Jamie Lynn put all things in perspective for him. He loved the way she loved him and he recognized it could only be divine and wanted to love her the same in return. He began to inquire about how to get that love. The answer came directly to him during the sermon when the preacher spoke of the love that God had for his only begotten son. The fact that Elijah had brought numerous people together who were broken in spirit translated to Lance that maybe God did care about him and had a plan for his life that was not his own.

As the choir glorified the Lord in psalms of Tramaine Hawkin's *"Goin' Up Yonder,"* the visiting guests participated in the processional around the church to pay their final respect to Elijah.

After making her way around the front of the church, Charlene immediately spotted Lydia and made it her business to approach her.

"Well hello there, Lydia. It has been a loooong time. I didn't even know you were still living around these parts. You must have a new address and phone number." Charlene sarcastically remarked and flashed her freshly cut diamond ring in her face to get her attention. They constantly maintained a friendly competition between the two of them ever since they were small children. Charlene was fairly more attractive than Lydia and received most of the attention from the boys around the neighborhood. Lydia despised that part about her. Lydia was no ugly woman, but she often fell into the shadows when Charlene came on the scene. For Lydia, she yearned to beat Charlene in something. They competed in fashion and even school. However, once Charlene met Edmond, she began to drift away from Lydia, choosing her man over her best friend.

"Char, stop all the nonsense! I called you several times, and you ignored me. However, I am glad to see you are doing well. Are you still with that no-good-of-a-man Edmond?" she rolled her eyes, ignoring all attempts for her to acknowledge her shiny ring she kept forcing in her face.

"I sure am. In fact, we are renewing our vows in the next couple of months. You should come to the ceremony. That is, if you are not too busy." Charlene requested, genuinely wanting her presence there. The time that had been lost within their time apart seemed minimal now that they were reconnected.

"Send me an invitation. I would love to come! You and Ed have come a long way, especially with the Raquel hiccups, but I am glad to see you are happy. Lord knows every woman deserves happiness."

"Mama, I'm about to get out of here and take Jamie Lynn home to change before we go to Mrs. Naples' house for the repast. Are you OK? Do you need anything?" Lance requested, gently embracing her from behind. He didn't even acknowledge the woman she was engaging with. His time was limited and Jamie Lynn kept complaining during the service about being hungry and he needed to see to it that she was taken care of.

"Mama?" Charlene questioned, her face crumpled up in confusion. This was definitely headline news to her ears. She was clueless about any form of pregnancy. The last experience she shared with her friend with regard to pregnancy had been when Lydia agreed to be her surrogate years ago. The In vitro fertilization attempt was unsuccessful, and she didn't hear much from her after.

"Hold up one moment, Lance. I want to introduce you to someone." She presented her son before Charlene, who couldn't help but feel an immediate connection to him. "Lance, this is an old friend of mine, Charlene Tucker. She is Edmond's wife." She stated, putting emphasis on Edmond's wife to remind him of exactly who she was connected to.

"Oh! You are Charles' Pops' wife? It's nice to meet you." He offered his hand to her.

"You are a very handsome young man. How old are you?"

Charlene asked inquisitively with a raised eyebrow.

"I'm twenty-seven." Lance stood firm with his shoulders back, feeling like a grown man in her presence.

"Oh, really? Who is the lucky man that is your father?" Charlene glanced over to Lydia to read her inner thoughts and glanced back over at Lance, inspecting him from head to toe. She shook her head and shrugged off where her thoughts were taking her. *It's impossible. It can't be!* She thought to herself. *No. She wouldn't do that.*

"Well, Mrs. Tucker, it was nice meeting you." He stepped in closer and whispered in Lydia's ear. "Mama, I'm gonna get out of here. I will stop by the house later to check on you. And thanks again for hooking me up with Jamie." He kissed Lydia on her cheek and exited the sanctuary.

"I know what you might be thinking, Charlene, and he is not your son. I got pregnant a few months later after the procedure didn't take. I didn't want to call you because I knew you wouldn't take it well. Besides, you were caught up in all the Edmond drama, and I honestly didn't want to be involved. Also for your information, his father left a long time ago. As fast as he came into my life, he was out of my life." Lydia responded, hoping it would be enough to get her off of her case.

"Sure you didn't. It doesn't matter, anyway. I have two beautiful children right over there and I'm finally at a place of happiness." She glanced over at Debra and Samson and smiled. At this point, she was content with it all. "Let me get your information, so I can send you that invite." They exchanged numbers and vowed to keep in contact.

Since her interaction with Lydia went smoothly and she was in the spirit of forgiveness, Charlene made her way around to the opposite side of the sanctuary to Raquel to smooth things over. There were still a few people left in the church, making it the best time to get a few words in. She needed her to first and foremost understand that Edmond would no longer be her go-to man for help anymore. Raquel also needed her to know that the agreement that for so long loomed over her head, that kept her in silence, was lifted and no longer an issue in her world.

"Excuse me, Raquel." Charlene lightly tapped Raquel on her shoulder. She sat quietly on the pew and didn't shift her body in Charlene's direction. She merely stared straight and briefly nodded to acknowledge her presence. "I am truly sorry for your loss. But it was going to happen sooner or later." Raquel maintained her posture, eyes locked on the view ahead of her. She didn't want to allow Charlene to get in her head with her wild antics and jabber. Charlene continued, unfazed by her stoic demeanor. "The life he lived was reckless and I am sure whoever did this to Calvin was just as dirty as he was." Raquel slightly shifted her body again in reaction to her obliviousness. It hit her at that moment that she had no clue as to the events that led up to his death. Charlene was just as out of the loop as always. In her mind, Edmond still didn't trust her enough to let her all the way in.

Raquel coughed in her hands and cleared her throat as she eased out a "Thank you."

"Let me get straight to the point. I really want to thank you for loving Edmond the way you did. Believe it or not, the relationship that carried on between you and my husband under my nose and behind my back put a lot of things in perspective for me. I was selfish at times. But now I see the error of my ways and ultimately, I got the better part of Ed, and I have *you* to thank for that."

Raquel slowly turned an acute angle degree, took a deep breath and swallowed hard. "I thank God I have grown. Although I want to reach out and touch you in the worse way; I won't give you that satisfaction because we are in God's house. I lost my cool at the salon the other day, so I apologize for that; but Ed will forever be in my life whether you like it or not, ring or no ring. Let's just agree to be cordial with one another." Charlene gave her a slight smile and patted her on her shoulder as to patronize her response. "As soon as the wedding glow wears off, he'll be back trying to rekindle old flames. Do you know where he was last night?" Raquel shot back under her breath.

"I know what you are trying to do, and I'm not falling for it this time." Charlene applied her best effort to maintain her composure and show Raquel that she didn't matter to her any longer. The words that so frequently used to ruffle her feathers would not faze her, she took a deep strong breath in to steady her breathing. *What do I have to worry about?* She thought to herself. *Edmond is mine. He loves me. He comes home to me. He pays my bills. He takes care of my children!* As her thoughts rapidly cut through her subconscious, she lost control. "If you ever touch my man again..."

"Charlene, you are a joke! You stepped into the picture, not me. Remember, I have been here!" Raquel shouted, interrupting her thought.

"Mama, it's time to go!" I interjected, to stop the madness before it began.

I saw the look in my mama's eyes. It took every fiber in her body to just grit her teeth and smile instead of going upside of Raquel's head. I knew from the moment I laid eyes on her in the sanctuary that the woman was touched, lonely and desperate. *A*

*Drama Queen.* Now, I also know that my mama is not blameless. She brought the entire situation upon herself, but whatever she felt she would gain from speaking with Raquel was a lost cause. I felt it my duty to my mother to step in.

"No, Debra! I have been walking away for far too long! This stops today!"

Raquel was now out of her seat and in my mother's face. "Let me be clear, Charlene, Ed came a-knocking plenty of nights and I turned him away because I didn't like the feeling of being the other woman. I knew you all had a family and believe-it-or-not, I wanted *your* kids to have the opportunity to have their father present. I don't know what kind of woman you think I am, but I do have a heart." She took in a deep breath, released and continued. "Yes, there were times when I was weak and I needed someone to hold me. However, if you think I am going to let you come in my face with this nonsense, you have got it all wrong. If you forgive Ed, then you forgive me! Don't be the typical bitter woman who tries to take her frustrations out on the woman because you don't have the gall to take it up with your own man."

The sanctuary lay quiet. Without noticing, their voices had escalated into yelling and everyone in the church was a spectator to the argument.

"What can I say? You're right!" I couldn't believe my ears. My mother conceded.

Edmond conveniently left himself out of the conversation. He heard them talking and convinced Samson to go out to the car with him just in the heat of the moment. He knew his wife was still capable of stirring the pot about matters that were now irrelevant. If he even attempted to step in between the two ladies, they might turn on him. His past experiences and wisdom taught him to stay out of the way when women were bickering. Eventually, they will come to a solution and a conclusion, which most likely would end up on his doorstep or through his pockets, anyway.

I wanted to point the blame at Raquel, then at my father; but after much thought, I realized we were all broken. We took the pain from one situation and carried it into the next; hoping that the next person would fix it, would take fault in the matter and give the release. Everyone who stepped foot in that sanctuary suffered from pain beyond their control. All of us wanted to move beyond the hurt to a place where we could just live and be liberated in the moment. Some found their refuge in God that day. For others, the seed was planted by the preached word. Others failed to tap in and missed the opportunity. My eyes were opened. I could see clearly just what the enemy was doing, and I refused to allow it to consume my family.

"Mama, I know that Black people don't normally do this, but we need to all go to therapy. I met this extremely nice White lady who will render us services for free." We laughed and embraced. All the people were making their way toward the exits as the deacons flickered the lights to let us know that it was past time to go. All seemed to be well for now.

Just as we stepped foot out of the church, a flood of cop cars came speeding up the street and surrounded the church steps. Five officers immediately hopped out and drew their guns. One overly eager officer announced to the crowd, signaling out my brother. "Samson Tucker, put your hands up! Don't make any sudden movements. You are under arrest for the murder of Calvin Rogers."

199

# Epilogue

The fear in everyone's faces told the story of how much we all didn't trust the police. They were there to protect and serve, but too many young Black boys were killed in the heat of the moment because they posed a threat to authorities. No one moved. Samson lifted his hands and gradually stepped closer to the police officer.

"Stop right there. Don't move. Keep your hands in plain sight where I can see them."

"What is going on with my baby?" Charlene glanced over to Edmond for answers. She recalled the confession of her son killing a young man, but he did it under the guidance of Calvin Rogers. "Edmond, what is going on?" She wanted to run to the aid of her little boy, but she knew it was impossible.

"You are under arrest for the murder of Calvin Rogers." With raised guns, three of the officers quickly moved in. They placed the handcuffs on his wrists and read him his rights.

From the funeral straight to the police station, we opted out of attending the interment to immediately see about Samson downtown. My mother and father waited around in the lobby, while I decided to poke my nose around to see what I could find out. I overheard a few of the officers discussing how they found Samson's DNA at the crime scene. I guess he was nervous and threw up and didn't think to clean it up. Evidence of his belongings were found in Calvin's vehicle. Let's face it. He wasn't a professional at killing people and covering it up. The most he knew was how to wipe his prints off the gun, which is what he saw on television. However, little did he know that, even that, was not foolproof. They tested Calvin's blood and crossed it with Samson's DNA sample. The next statement shattered my existence.

"What would possess this boy to kill his father?" the officer asked his partner, disgusted at how the world turned so evil.

"It's a cold game. He probably wanted to take over his empire." The officer responded, chuckling and shaking his head in disappointment.

*His father? What in the world? Never! Did Samson know that Calvin Rogers was his father and plotted to kill him?* Nothing about the scenario seemed right. I began to question everything. I was under the impression, from my mother's confession, that my father was the unfaithful one. My mother managed to carry this secret for this long and still point the finger at my daddy. Then I thought about it more. *What if she never knew? What if my mother, in a wild rage, spent a drunken night with Calvin to get back at Raquel and my dad?* It all became too much to bear. If it was a secret, it would remain that way. Therapy and plenty of Jesus became more and more of an urgency for us. We had a lot of sins that needed forgiving.

I joined my parents back in the waiting room. The investigator came out to let us know it would be a couple of hours before we would know anything for certain. I decided to go back to the car and get my laptop to start the narrative assignment for my English class. For some odd reason, I was feeling extremely inspired to write.

# About the Author

Sharifa "Akilah Trinay" Norris is truly a unique soul. As one of the co-host of U Nation Radio's "Monday Night Love Sessions," she brings sexy sophistication to Internet radio. Akilah Trinay was born and raised in Oakland, CA and despite the fact that she has relocated to Los Angeles; "The Bay" will always be home to her. She graduated from California State University, Los Angeles with a B.A. in Communications with an emphasis in Public Relations.

She briefly worked in radio, television and public relations before transitioning her aspirations toward education. She went on to earn her M. Ed. from Alliant International University. By day, Sharifa Norris is an educator and advocate for student achievement and by night, Akilah Trinay is the essence of the modern day Renaissance woman, evoking stimulating conversation and self-reflection. Through this endeavor, she was inspired to write her first novel "Beyond the Hurt".

**You can connect with me on:**

🌐 https://www.revisionpub.com
📘 https://www.facebook.com/revisionpub